High Tide

by P. M. Hubbard

"P. M. Hubbard has a certain touch of magic in evoking dark, dank terror."

—*The New York Times Book Review*

P. M. HUBBARD

HIGH TIDE

PERENNIAL LIBRARY
Harper & Row, Publishers
New York, Cambridge, Philadelphia, San Francisco
London, Mexico City, São Paulo, Sydney

A hardcover edition of this book was originally published by Atheneum Publishers. It is here reprinted by arrangement.

First PERENNIAL LIBRARY edition published 1982.

ISBN 0-06-080571-4

82 83 84 85 86 10 9 8 7 6 5 4 3 2 1

HIGH TIDE

CHAPTER 1

I PUT MY HAND OUT and waved the other car past. I did not want to be rushed, and I was in no particular hurry to get anywhere, if only because I was not very sure where I was. The car passed me, putting its off-side wheels over the edge of the tarmac and raising a small cloud of dust as long as they were there. The dust swirled about in the air eddies raised by the two cars, and then, as I watched it in my driving mirror, hung about over the road, settling slowly. There was no natural movement in the air at all. Even at this time of the morning the sun-heat was all the weather that mattered. It was all very un-English.

But I was not out of England yet. Even if I was not very sure where I was, I knew that all along a line twenty or so miles south of me the Channel lay covered with a flat sheen under the slightly misted sky. I knew just what it would look like under these conditions. They did happen occasionally, and when they did, you remembered them. I had not actually seen the Channel for nearly five years.

I also knew that the place where the whole business had begun was now about thirty miles behind me. I had passed a few miles south of it during the night, and now it was away east of me. I had planned my course to miss it, and now I had. Now I was edging south towards the sea as I drove westwards. I wondered whether it would not have been better to go there and look at it, but at any rate I had not, and now it was behind me and getting further away every minute.

The other car did not seem in any hurry to get away. It was the first I had seen that morning. I had waved it through as soon as I saw it behind me, but it was still there, going my pace fifty or so yards ahead. I had not even noticed who was in it, but it irritated me, and I wanted it out of the way. I pulled in under a bunch of trees and stopped. The other car rolled sedately away and disappeared over the top of the hill. After that nothing moved at all except the birds, and they darted furtively from tree to tree, cutting their flying time down to whatever minimum met their immediate needs. They sang occasionally out of the shade, but tentatively, as if they found the silence too much to cope with.

I sat there in the car, taking it all in. It seemed an unnecessary complication that when the country was in any case, after all these years, unfamiliar, it should also happen to be so untypical. It made the whole experience doubly strange.

But I liked the silence. Above all, I liked the silence and the solitude, just as at night I liked the darkness. The trouble with prison was the same as with hospitals and I suppose boarding schools and any other institution where you have a number of mainly unwilling inmates looked after by a small staff. It was never entirely quiet or entirely dark, and even if you were supposed to be alone, you never felt it. There was always a light burning round a corner or someone talking at the far end of a corridor. That was why I was travelling the way I was, driving at night and in the early mornings and lying up during the day. I had come all the way down from the north like that. Whatever it looked like, it had nothing to do with being furtive. I had no reason to be furtive. I was a free man with money of my own. It puzzled the hotels a bit, of course. They were so used to bed and breakfast that breakfast and bed took some explaining. But there was nothing they could get upset about, once they understood that I was not in some way trying to do them out of some payment they felt entitled to. So I travelled, as far as I could, through a silent and empty England, mostly in the darkness, but using as much of the early mornings as I needed to get to the next hotel open and ready to take me in. I took it very easy, pulling up for a rest at some point every night. Already I felt unbelievably the better for it.

There was traffic on the main road by the time I got to it, mainly heavy stuff. I thought it was time I got off it. The signpost said Burton St. Michael 9 miles, and I decided that if Burton St. Michael had a hotel, that would be it. There was a car parked on the side of the road where I turned out, but I was watching for the lorries and took no particular notice of it. I drove on, faster now. The early-morning exhilaration had worn off, and I was getting sleepy.

The odd thing is that I cannot now remember the name of the hotel, but it was the only one, and it looked all right. Burton St. Michael turned out to be a large village strung out along the road. There were several pubs, but only one had developed into a hotel catering for the road business. The front door was open and the place smelt fresh. There was no one at the desk, but the drone of a vacuum cleaner led me to a woman in a pink overall. A local woman, I thought, with a husband gone early to work. The overall would be hotel uniform, more or less. I was still passionately interested in women, not only their sex, but everything about them. I told her what I wanted, and she switched off the cleaner and said, "I'll tell Miss Benton."

Miss Benton had been called away from her breakfast, but she did not seem to mind. She seemed pleased to see me. That was one of the things I still could not get used to, being welcome. Not but what I looked all right, better, almost certainly, than four years ago. I said, "I've been driving all night, and I think it's time I got some sleep. I wonder if you can find me a room? At the back, if possible."

I had got the approach worked out now, and Miss Benton even took the second line of the script out of my hands. She said, "Yes, that will be all right, sir. You'd like some breakfast first, I expect."

"Oh yes, please," I said. I signed where she showed me and put my bank address.

"I'll put you in Number Six," she said. "It's small, but it's over the garden. You'll be quiet there."

I said, "That will be fine," and went out to put the car away and get my bags.

When I came in again, Miss Benton had disappeared, but the overalled woman took me over. She was older, the mothering sort. She was not going to call anyone of my age sir. She said, "Been driving all night, Miss Benton said. You'll be tired."

"I am a bit. But nothing that a few hours' sleep won't cure. Many people in?"

She looked at me as if she found this funny. "Not coming in at this time of the morning," she said. "There'll be two going out after breakfast, and I expect more coming in this evening. When are you going on, then?"

Motherly or not, I did not want to discuss my movements with her. "I'll see what I feel like," I said.

She was faintly curious, and I wondered, as I spent a good deal of time wondering, whether she noticed anything and whether there was anything to notice. If there was, she could not put her finger on it, and motherliness reasserted itself. "That's right," she said. "You get a good sleep, and you'll feel better. You'll be quite quiet here."

Number Six was a small cool room with just about gangway between the bed and the rest of the furniture. The window was open, and the garden underneath still had the faint early-morning smell, with the sun not yet on it. I looked at it all with enormous pleasure. The woman said, "Breakfast will be ready in ten minutes, Miss Benton said."

"That's fine," I said. "I'll be down."

She hung for a moment in the doorway and then gave it up. She said, "Right-oh then," and went off down the passage, leaving the door open. I shut it and opened the only case that mattered. When I came upstairs again, I leant out of the window for a moment, snuffing up the scents of the garden. But my breakfast had made me sleepy. I shut the window firmly, in case the birds got out of hand, or someone started in with a lawn-mower. The curtains were flowery but solid, and kept out a lot of light. I drew them close and got undressed and washed in the slightly coloured dusk. When I got into bed, I could just hear the vacuum cleaner droning away somewhere in the bottom of the house, but I rather liked it. It was a very domestic sort of noise. It made me feel, in a not very explicit sort of way, that someone in a pink overall was looking after me. I went to sleep almost at once.

I drifted awake a little after three. The house was dead quiet, and I lay for a bit savouring the silence and my physical comfort. Then I got up and opened the window, leaving the curtains drawn. The sun was coming round to the back of the house and the room would soon be getting warm. Even the birds had almost given up now. Only an occasional chirp showed that they were still there. The dead weight of that extraordinary summer weather lay on the garden, and nothing stirred under it.

I had had all the sleep I wanted. I got dressed in a leisurely sort of way and went downstairs, hoping I might find someone who would give me tea. There was no one about. The hotel register still lay open on the desk where I had signed it early in the morning. I was going past it when a single line of rather black writing caught my eye. I stopped and went over to look at it. There was another entry after mine. Somebody called C. W. Matthews had clocked in during the day and had been given Room Number Four. Mr. Matthews was British and lived in Surbiton, which did not promise any great excitement. The only thing which interested me was the fact that the woman in the pink overall had been wrong when she had said that there would be no one in until the evening. I did not know when Mr. Matthews had arrived, but whatever had brought him to Burton St.

Michael, it had brought him there fairly early in the day. He was not the ordinary overnight visitor. Whether he too had retired to bed I did not know, and short of going up and knocking on the door of Number Four, I had no means of finding out.

I did not want to disturb the peace by ringing the bell on the desk, and in any case I had a feeling that no one would hear it if I did. I wandered down a passage going towards the back of the house and tapped on a likely-looking door. The woman in the kitchen was neither Miss Benton nor the woman in the pink overall, but she knew who I was. I thought she had probably seen me at breakfast, and people remember me, if only because of my size. She took my suggestion of tea with calm, and said would I like it in the garden? I said, "Oh yes, please," and went out to wait for it.

It was not much, I suppose, but I was enormously pleased by it. Things like this, gratuitous offers of small considerations, still took me by the throat with their unexpected kindness. I sat down on a white-painted bench under the shade of a May tree, feeling almost dangerously happy. I was aware of the danger underneath the happiness. I think it gave it an extra tang. The danger was that the happiness would not last. That is a threat common to all sorts of happiness, but here there were two good reasons for it which even I could see. The first was the obvious one that things might be different if people knew about me. I was not entirely sure of this, but I think I had been led to assume it. For all I really knew, the woman in the pink overall might be more motherly, not less, if she knew I had just come out of prison; but I did not think so. The odd thing was that I badly wanted to tell her.

The second reason was just that my present happiness was too simple to last. It was the merest happiness of normal human relations and ordinary living, and there are very few people who can keep happy for long on that. No doubt you ought to be able to, but civilisation, or something, makes it next to impossible. At the moment I was utterly content, but sooner or later I should start to want something I had not got. Meanwhile, I was aware of the insecurity of my happiness and at the same time consciously tempted to put it at risk.

When the woman brought out the tray, I thought of ways of telling her why I was as pleased with it as I was, but before I could choose the right words, she had put the tray down and gone back into the house. That left only the birds, and they were no use. I fell back on the solid substance of my insecure content. There was bread-and-butter in not over-thin slices and home-made jam and cakes. I ate it all with the sort of pleasure I had not known since childhood. When I had finished, I walked round the garden, dodging back into the shade whenever I got too hot. Then I went upstairs to my room and lay on my still unmade bed in the flowered dusk behind the drawn curtains, waiting for dinner and the time to be on the move again.

Mr. Matthews apart, the woman in the pink overall had been right. There were two parties of obvious travellers at dinner, a pair of commercial gentlemen of a fairly familiar type and a young couple with two small children. The two children were full of the excitement of holiday travel and the parents a bit edgy with the strain of it. They made more noise between them than the rest of us put together. The businessmen talked to each other steadily in earnest undertones. Mr. Matthews was recognisable at once, if only because he was so startlingly ordinary. If you had been asked to imagine a typical Surbiton man, you would have imagined something very like Mr. Matthews. Everything about him was discreet, his dark suit, his glasses, his voice when he spoke to the waitress, even his choice of food and the way he ate it. I could not see him as a fly-by-night like myself. His table was next to mine. He was already there when I came in, and nodded pleasantly. I nodded back.

I did not think discretion would allow him further familiarities, but in this I was wrong. We finished our meal and got up to go almost together, and as we got near the door he ventured a cautious smile. "Been a wonderful day," he said.

"Wonderful," I said.

We went out into the hall together. He said, "I don't know—I was thinking of having a night-cap. Would you care to join me?"

I hesitated, but I should be away from Burton St. Michael in an hour's time, and I saw no harm in it. "Yes," I said, "I'd like that very much."

He nodded. "Good," he said. "The bar's in here."

He ordered a couple of whiskies, and we both filled them to the top with soda. It was a hot evening, and I was every bit as discreet as he was. "It's warm in here," he said. "Shall we take them in the garden?"

I said, "That would be nice," and meant it. I rather took to Mr. Matthews. He was so gentle and diffident. We went out into the dusk and settled ourselves on the white-painted bench under the May tree. There was night-scented stock somewhere in the garden, and the place smelt as near paradise as one has a right to expect, even in the West Country.

"Going far?" he said. He seemed to assume I was a traveller. I suppose not many people actually stayed in Burton St. Michael. It was nice enough, but there was nothing much to stay for.

"I'm going westwards," I said.

He nodded. "Business or pleasure?"

"Purely pleasure."

"You're lucky," he said. "I'm on business myself."

I suddenly found my heart beating faster, but there we were, in that paradisal garden, and he had paid for the drinks. I could not just get up and go. I sat there, sipping my drink and telling myself it was all nonsense. He said, "I'm looking into the affairs of a late colleague of mine." I knew then, without a shadow of doubt, that it was going to happen, and it did. "A man called Evan Maxwell," he said.

"I see," I said.

He was looking into his glass, turning it round and round in his hand. Then he looked up. "You knew him, perhaps?" he said.

"My acquaintance with him was very brief."

"So I gathered. Nevertheless, I think you might be able to help me."

"In what way?"

He thought for a moment, looking down at what was left of his drink. Then he drank it off and put the empty glass down on the bench beside him. He said, "Look, Mr. Curtis, it's all quite a long time ago now. So far as you're concerned, it's all finished and done with."

I said, "So I had hoped."

"So it is," he said. "For you, but not for me. That was why I hoped you might be able to help me."

Like him, I finished my drink and put my glass down. "All right," I said, "tell me what it is you want."

CHAPTER 2

He said, "I want to know everything that happened during your, as you say, brief acquaintance with him."

"But I said all that at the trial. I said—"

"I know what you said at the trial, of course. But I've assumed it was not complete. Or even, indeed, very accurate. One doesn't expect completeness or accuracy from a man in your position. I mean the position you were in then. Now your position is quite different."

"I see. I'm afraid I must ask you to declare your interest, Mr. Matthews. I'm sorry if I deprived you of a colleague, but I must know which side you're on. If Maxwell was a friend of yours—"

Mr. Matthews interrupted me. He did it, as he did everything, with gentleness and discretion, but quite effectively. He said, "Evan Maxwell was the most God-awful bastard I ever knew." Coming in his gentle, precise little voice, this gave me enormous and immediate relief. It was something I had always known, but had never been able to make anyone say, because it was not supposed to be relevant. It was not, in fact, relevant to the matters the court had to decide. In some system of higher justice I think it might have been, but not at law. The fact that it would have been a considerable comfort to me to have the thing recognised was neither here nor there. No one, at that particular time, was concerned with my comfort, only with punishing me for what I had done. I did not dispute the propriety of this, but it was galling, nevertheless, never to hear that key fact stated.

All I said was, "Ah."

"I don't mind telling you," said Mr. Matthews, "that if you had needed it, there were some of us who would have been ready to help you when—well, now, I mean."

"When I came out?"

"Exactly, yes. But we found on enquiry that you did not need help—I mean, not in that particular kind of way."

"I see," I said. "That was no doubt kind of you. I have in fact an income of sorts, and of course it has been accumulating."

"Just so. However, the possibility remains that you might be able to help us."

I said, "I doubt it, but I'll try if you like. On conditions, of course."

He nodded. "What would your conditions be?"

"Well—it's only one condition, really. It's this. There must be no reopening of the matter, at least so far as I am concerned. The whole thing's been forgotten—by most people, anyhow. It wasn't a particularly interesting case to start with. A momentary heart-throb for the great animal-loving British public, but nothing else. The story was dead twenty-four hours after the trial, or so I was assured. It's got to stay dead. Until a couple of minutes ago I thought I was a free man—I mean, free that way. I still intend to remain so."

There was a faint glow of light from the windows at the back of the hotel, and even under the shadow of the May tree I could see Mr. Matthews' face well enough to know what he was at. He was looking at me very intently. For a moment he just looked. Then he said, "Why this travelling by night, then?"

This made me angry. I get angry very quickly. That had been the trouble all along. My reasons for travelling at night had been innocent, and private, and perhaps rather foolish. I did not in the least want to have to explain them. I said, "Damn you, that's none of your business."

As I might have known, Mr. Matthews was not an easy man to get angry with. He considered this calmly. He even seemed rather doubtful. "It's not?" he said.

I gave it up. "Look," I said, "have you ever spent four years in jail?"

"I'm afraid not." He seemed rather apologetic about it.

"Well, were you ever at a public school?"

He laughed, quietly, as he did everything, but disconcertingly. "Of a sort," he said. "Nothing very distinguished, I'm afraid."

"All right. Now suppose you had had to stay at school for four years continuously, not just twelve weeks at a time, or whatever it was. How do you think you'd have felt when they finally let you out?"

He nodded again. "I see," he said. "At least, I think I see. I admit I hadn't thought of it like that."

"Well, try. I was never much more than an amateur jail-bird, at best. I fought very hard, in fact, to preserve my amateur status. The main ingredient is mental privacy. I must have that. The fact that I was obviously capable of fighting for what I wanted of course helped. Now I thought I had it without having to fight for it. Until I met you, that is. As it is, I shall continue to have it, even if I have once more to fight for it. Well, Mr. Matthews?"

This, too, he considered for quite a time. Then he said, "I think you are a dangerous man, Mr. Curtis. But I suppose, on the record, that might be expected. I still have to deal with you. All right. I accept your explanation. This must also, I suppose, account for the fact that you already knew my name when I spoke to you just now?"

"I saw your name in the register, of course. But yes—in a sort of way I think it does."

"Very well. Now—will you accept my assurance that if you will give me the information I need, you will not see me again and will hear nothing more of the matter—I mean, not from me?"

"What if I don't?"

"Well—you are, even on your own account, in a somewhat vulnerable position, aren't you?"

We looked at each other in the faint light. He looked as mild and deprecating as ever, but I did not feel at all the same about him. "What do you want me to do?" I said.

"Just tell me what happened. Everything that happened during those few minutes before the other car came along."

I said, "I had a dog." I had never tried doing this, not in all these years. I listened to my own voice in a curious, detached sort of way, as if someone had cut off a part of myself and I was looking at it, lying there in front of me. "He was a good dog, and I was very fond of him. We were on that road—you know where it was. He had run into a field on the other side of the road and I called him back. He came rolling back across the road, with his tail flagging in time, grinning all over his face. You know what Labradors are. Marxwell came round the bend in his Jaguar, doing God knows what and well on his wrong side. The dog never had a chance. One thing, he was killed quickly. There was—there was quite a bang. They're heavy dogs, you know. Maxwell stopped the car about thirty yards down the road."

Mr. Matthews said, "That wasn't like him."

"He was angry," I said. "I think he thought he'd damaged his car."

He nodded. "Go on," he said.

"When I came up with him, he said, 'Why don't you keep your dog under control? It might have killed me.' He was looking up at me out of the open window of his car. I said, 'I shouldn't worry. I'm going to do that anyhow.' "

He nodded. He seemed even quietly amused. He said, "I can understand your not telling that to the police. Were you, in fact?"

"I shouldn't think so. I don't really cut loose. I just lose my temper a bit. It doesn't last."

"I see. Well?"

"He was frightened. I can tell you that, seeing that he was no friend of yours. He was as scared as hell. He saw his death coming, all right, even if he misjudged the details. I hit him through the open window. You can't hit very hard like that, obviously, but I hit him hard enough. I hit him right in the middle of his face. His nose bled like a tap, and he fell back against the seat. I opened the door and put my hands on his throat. I squeezed it a bit, but I wasn't trying to strangle him, not by then. The worst was over by then. The dog was dead, anyway. I squeezed his throat and told him what I felt about him and what he had done. That was the thing, do you see? I had to make him understand what he'd done. Then he had—I don't know, some sort of convulsion. His whole body jerked. I took my hands off his throat. He was quite alive, but his eyes were shut, and he looked bad. I pulled him out of the car and put him down on the grass at the side of the road. He was there, with me kneeling by him, when the other car came along. But by then he was dead."

"How long after was that?"

"I don't know, of course. A few minutes."

"And most of that time he was alive?"

"Oh yes. He had his eyes open by then and was looking up at me."

"What did he say?"

"Say? I don't think—" My mind checked at that, as if it was something I ought to be able to answer and could not. "I don't remember," I said. "I think—I think he did talk a little, because that was how I knew he was alive. His eyes stared so much you couldn't tell. But I can't remember what he said. It's a long time ago, you know, and I was in a bit of a state by then. I don't think he did much more than mutter. All I remember is that I knew he was alive because he was talking, or trying to talk, and then he stopped and I knew he was dead. The eyes didn't change. I was wondering what the hell to do, when the other car came along. I suppose if I'd known he had a weak heart—but I didn't, of course."

He said, "They allowed for that. All the same, I thought the sentence a stiff one."

"I had been in trouble before," I said. "Same sort of thing, but the chap could take it. I told you. I get angry. And I'm very strong, of course."

He nodded again. "Yes," he said, "that was it. I suppose the judge wasn't far wrong, really."

"So I was advised."

There was a moment's silence. Then Mr. Matthews leant forward a little. He was staring into my face all the time in the faint reflected light, and now he leant forward, so that his eyes seemed only a foot or so away from mine. "Think," he said. "Try to remember. This is of the utmost importance. Try to think back. If you remember his talking, you must be able to remember what he said."

I stared back at him, and in my mind I saw the pale face and the wide hazel eyes staring up at me from the grass at the side of the road. I remembered the mouth, too. The lips were rather thick, and gaped a little. There was blood all round them from his punched nose. Then they shut and opened again, and he said something. But I did not know what. I shook my head. "It's no good," I said. "It didn't seem important at the time. It was what had happened that was important. And I suppose I've buried the thing a bit in my mind. Not because of Maxwell. I couldn't care less about Maxwell. Because of the dog. I haven't really thought about it for God knows how long. Now you've brought it up, I feel—I don't know, I feel I ought to be able to remember. But I can't. I'm sorry."

Mr. Matthews leant back again, but said nothing.

"You do believe me?" I said.

There was another moment's silence, and then he sighed. It was a long sigh. I suppose he sighed at the disappointment of a long hope. He just nodded.

I said, "Perhaps if you'll tell me what it is you're after— Can you give me some suggestion of what you think he might have said? I might at least be able to reject it."

But he shook his head.

I got up. "At that rate," I said, "there doesn't seem anything more for us to talk about. Perhaps you'll excuse me now, Mr. Matthews. I want to get started."

He stayed where he was on the white bench. The May tree grew so low that I stooped a little as I stood over him. "Where are you going?" he said. "You've passed the place where it happened. I thought perhaps you were making for there. It was when I saw you weren't that I decided to speak to you."

"I don't know, exactly. I think down to the south coast. South Cornwall, or something of the sort. I want to buy a boat. Something big enough to live on but not too big to sail single-handed. Then I'll cruise for a bit. Completely on my own, do you see? No solitude like the solitude on a boat. Only coastal stuff, I think. To start with, anyhow. Later I'll see."

He said, "France, perhaps?"

"Perhaps. Why?"

He shrugged. "The next place you come to," he said.

I did not think he had really finished with me. But he did not ask any more questions. He still did not get up. He just sat there, with his empty glass beside him and his hands clasped between his knees, staring in front of him. He almost seemed to have forgotten I was there. I said, "There's one thing I don't understand. Why do you think Maxwell would have talked at all—I mean, said anything of importance? Why to me, of all people?"

He spoke without looking up, so that I had the feeling that he was seeing Maxwell in his mind's eye, as I had just seen him, and not me at all. "Because he was like that," he said. "You didn't know him, of course. He talked all the time. The audience didn't matter, and the voice didn't vary much. Unless he was deliberately deceiving you, he really did do his thinking aloud. Much of it wasn't nice, because he wasn't a nice person. But if there was anything urgent on his mind, it might well have come out, whatever state he was in, so long as he could talk at all."

"And there was something urgent on his mind?"

He hesitated, but saw no way round it. He looked up at me then. "Oh yes," he said. "Maxwell was on very urgent business when you stopped him, you and your dog."

"If you know it was that urgent," I said, "I imagine you know what it was about. What is it you want to know, then? I suppose where he was going. Is that right? If so, I'm sorry I can't help you. You know where he was and which way he was heading. After that your guess must be a good deal better than mine." But even while I was talking, my mind began niggling again, as if there was something there, trying to get out, and one more small door had opened between me and it.

Mr. Matthews got up. "If I were you, Mr. Curtis," he said, "I'd put the whole thing out of your mind and go on with your cruising plans."

"I intend to. It was you who brought it back into my mind, wasn't it?"

"I know. But I don't think, in fact, that that will have done you any harm."

There was a touch of the earlier gentleness in his voice. I no longer believed him gentle, but I saw, nevertheless, that he was very likely right. Merely talking about it had loosened things up. It would, of course, only I had had no one to talk to. I had not chosen Mr. Matthews of Surbiton as my confessor, but that did not alter the fact that confession, whether or not it was good for the soul, certainly made it easier to live with. I wondered whether the loosening-up process would extend to the memory as well as the emotions, and whether this was a possibility that Mr. Matthews had considered. Knowing him as I now did, I did not think he would have missed it. He had urged me to put the matter out of my mind, but I doubted whether he would be content with that. I had the feeling, whatever he said, that he would not willingly let my mind far out of his sight just in case I did not. Perhaps this was what he was thinking about. He seemed to be thinking very hard about something when I left him and went back into the house.

I had made my explanations to Miss Benton earlier, and she had my bill ready at the desk. I paid it and brought my cases down. I did not see Mr. Matthews anywhere. I took my cases out to the car and ran the car out to the front of the hotel. Then I went back inside. It is always odd going back into a hotel after you have paid your bill and surrendered your key and left. The place is familiar, but you feel displaced in it. The staff look at you doubtfully, and your reappearance seems to need some explanation, especially if you go upstairs.

I went upstairs. Number Four was not far from Number Six. The door was shut and I could not hear anyone inside. I came downstairs again and went into the passage leading to the bar, where the telephone box was. Mr. Matthews was in the box, talking. He was as unexcited as ever, but he talked very earnestly. I knew then. I knew with an absolute certainty as I watched him that this was not the last of it. Through no fault of mine, because I had helped to kill the particular man I had, I was under surveillance again. Unless I was very lucky, I was in danger of paying twice. There was nothing I could do, because I did not seem able to give them the one thing they wanted from me. I was a sort of raw material, which had not proved as processable as they had hoped, but which could not be discarded. What frightened me was the possibility of further processing. When I had set myself to defend the privacy of my mind, it had not occurred to me that there might be something in my mind which other people wanted. It was as if I had inadvertently swallowed somebody's pet diamond, and only abdominal surgery would get it out. At that time I would gladly have parted with the diamond if it could be done without surgery. It was only later that I considered the possibility of keeping it for myself.

I went back into the hall. Miss Benton was no longer at the desk, and there was no one about. I went to the desk and opened the register. Like most hotel registers, it required you to enter the registration number of your car. I noted Mr. Matthews' and shut the book. I was half-way to the door when I heard someone coming along the passage from the bar. I went out of the door and stood in the darkness outside, looking back into the lighted hall. Mr. Matthews crossed the hall and went upstairs. His walk was unhurried and his expression as calm as ever. If he felt frustrated or upset, he did not show it. I had the idea that he had passed on his frustration to the person he had been talking to on the phone, but this was no more than a guess.

I went round to the garage and found his car. It was as undistinctive as the rest of him. It could perfectly well have been the car I had seen that morning on the road, but I could not pretend I recognised it. I got into my own car and set out westwards.

There was still a certain amount of traffic, but it was thinning out. I drove for half an hour before an idea occurred to me and I pulled in to the side of the road. I did not know if the idea was worth much, but time meant nothing to me, and it was at least worth trying. I waited till the road was clear. Then I swung the car round and drove back to Burton St. Michael. I stopped some way short of the hotel and walked the rest of the way.

Already the hotel had its night face on. There was a light in the hall, but most of the public rooms were dark. Two or three of the upstairs rooms had lights burning behind drawn curtains. The way round to the garage was open, and I walked round in the darkness. There was no one about. Mr. Matthews' car still stood where I had left it. I walked back to mine. Some lines from Housman came into my head.

But the city, dusk and mute,
Slept, and there was no pursuit.

Whatever I was up against, it was no longer Mr. Matthews. I turned the car and once more headed west.

CHAPTER 3

IT WAS SOMETHING TO DO with the sea. I remembered the incongruity of it, coming from that town-dressed man with his fast car and his puffy face. Something to do with the sea, I should get it in a moment. Then the afternoon light came flooding into my eyes, and I was fully awake. It was gone, whatever it was. But it was something to do with the sea. I rolled over in bed and sat up. The bed here was not as comfortable as it had been at Burton St. Michael, and the room was bigger and less charming. But I had slept well enough, and that was what mattered. It was a quarter to three. I was getting very regular in my irregular habits. I lay back again and stared at the ceiling.

I had thought about the thing while I was driving, but driving by night calls for more concentration than driving by day, and I had not thought very coherently. What I mainly remembered was that I had not minded thinking about it, or not nearly so much. The curious, steely sympathy of Mr. Matthews had not been misplaced. Telling him about it, even under duress, had undoubtedly done me good. I doubted now whether his name was really Matthews, and I did not at all believe that he came from Surbiton. I thought he had picked on Surbiton because it struck him, as it had struck me, as so disarming. I do not know what the crime figures are for Surbiton, but I should not expect them to be high. But wherever he had come from, he had done more than ease my mind. He had set my memory working. I remembered thinking, last night in that stock-scented garden, that this might be a secondary effect and wondering whether he might have the same idea. Whether he had or not, there it was.

I had been too busy with my driving, almost from the moment I left him, to do much conscious remembering, but somewhere in my mind I had been working on it, and even making some progress. I thought that, so long as I did not worry about it, the thing he thought he wanted would come to me sooner or later, and I wondered what I should do with it when I had it. The diamond I did not want was finding its own way out without surgery. Now that I came to think about it, the analogy was not an elegant one, but the problem was real. Or would be, when it arose. I had not got the diamond yet. Meanwhile, better think of something else, and the thing I thought of, naturally enough, was tea.

I sat up again. Then I got out of bed, pulled back the curtains and opened the window. I smelt the sea at once. I had not smelt it at all during the night, nor when I had got in early this morning. But it was near enough, and now some change of wind had brought the smell of it straight to me. There is no mistaking it and nothing at all like it. I wondered whether I should have felt like this, or even noticed it, if I had done my time in Parkhurst or some other reasonably maritime place of confinement. I came to the conclusion that I should have noticed it, because it is a thing you never lose once you have been brought up to it, but not reacted so violently. As it was, I put my hands on the window-sill and my head on my hands and cried quietly and cheerfully for a minute or two. Then I got dressed.

As I got dressed I went back to thinking about Mr. Matthews. I could see now that, looked at from his point of view, my actions since I came out might well suggest that I was off to make clandestine use of something I had learnt before I went in. In fact I knew I did not possess any information of that sort. Whatever it was I could not quite remember, it was not the hiding-place of the loot or the map reference of the gold-mine. Obviously, if it had been, I should not have forgotten it. Whatever the puffy mouth had said, it had not meant much to me at the time. Even if I had remembered it later, it would still never have occurred to me that it might have a value. It was Mr. Mathews' predicament that he had to try to find out what it was, but could not do this without letting me see that it might be valuable. I think it was when I reached this point in my thinking that the idea of keeping the diamond for myself first occurred to me. Only I still had not got it, and did not know, until I had, whether it was negotiable.

The weather still held, but there was no garden here, only a yard at the back where what had once been stables were now lock-up garages. It was a town hotel, though the town was a small one, even by West Country standards. But half past three is a pretty quiet time of day in most hotels. I met no one in the angled lengths of creaking corridor which the smaller English hotel still enjoys, and when I came out at the head of the shallow stairs, I could see no one in the hall below. Somewhere down there a clock ticked with the beautifully slow beat that spoke of a pendulum escapement, and a pretty long pendulum at that. Nothing else stirred. I went down the stairs and turned towards the front door. This of course took me past the reception desk, which was what I really had in mind. The register was spread out on the desk, and I looked into the rather dusky cubby-hole behind it. I could see no one there, and walked across to it. It was only when I got there that I saw the top of a girl's head. She was sitting at a low table, with her back half turned to me. There was paperwork spread out in front of her, but she was knitting busily.

The hall was carpeted. I leant over the desk and had what I wanted before she knew I was there. When she looked up, I saw that she was wonderfully pretty in a soft, countrified sort of way, but the flash of an engagement ring on her moving left hand told me that she was already bespoke. She said, "Oh, you startled me." She did not look in the least startled, only placidly aware of her own attractions.

I said, "Do you think I could have some tea?"

"Of course," she said, "I'll tell them. In the lounge?" It was not a word I liked, but the West Country diphthong robbed it of offence.

"In the lounge will be fine," I said. There was no entry under mine. No Mr. Matthews had booked in after me. I wandered off down the hall, and was suddenly aware of my disappointment. To my surprise, Mr. Matthews had done more than ease my heart and jog my memory. He had given me an interest in life. The world about me was still pretty pure paradise, but no paradise is complete without its snake. Or, I thought, without its Eve, but that could wait. My spell of enforced celibacy had produced the inevitable accumulation of feeling, but it had left me hesitant, perhaps diffident. The released convict who has himself driven straight to the nearest brothel must, I thought, be a man of blessedly simple mind. For myself, I found that even the possibility of the thing took quite a bit of getting used to. But this was for the moment irrelevant. What was important was the discovery that Mr. Matthews, and whatever it was he represented, was no longer a threat to my peace of mind, but even possibly a relish to my enjoyment of freedom.

I drank my tea in the silence of the lounge and wondered what would happen if I began to act out the part of the diamond thief. I had no doubt Mr. Matthews had accepted my failure to remember as genuine, because it had been genuine and I did not suppose he made many mistakes about things like that. Equally I did not think that he would overlook the possibility that I might remember something and be interested, now, in what I remembered. The more I thought about it, the more certain I felt that, whether or not I had seen the last of Mr. Matthews and his lot, they had not seen the last of me. I did not really think that my movements from now on would go unwatched, at least until I actually got aboard ship and out to sea.

The question was what I was going to do about this, now that I seemed to have got over my first blind instinct for escape. I came to the conclusion, over my third cup of tea, that I could not do anything much until I had my diamond. I put my cup down, brushed some crumbs off my lap and put the whole thing out of my mind. As I got up, I remembered that it was something to do with my car.

Just that, no more. Something to do with the sea, as I had already remembered, and also in some way to do with my car. What the connection was between the two I did not know. I tried to let my mind play casually with the idea of my car, but the difficulty was that it was not the same car as I had now. I had had it for only a very short time before the thing happened. Then it had been sold. Of all the cars I had had at one time or another, it was the one I remembered least about. I was going to be very lucky if, of the little I remembered, my mind turned up the bit I wanted.

I went down a passage and out of the back door into the yard. This was in any case the best time to look over the car before the night's run, and now I had an extra interest in her. Even if she was not the same car, something about her might give me the clue I wanted. All cars, at least the sort of cars I bought, were much the same these days.

I did the usual checks, ran the car out, filled her up at the nearest pump and put her back in the yard again. Nothing occurred to me, but the great thing was not to worry about it. There was no smell of the sea now. Whatever wind had brought it was gone, and the air was motionless and so heavy that it seemed difficult to breathe. The sky overhead was hazy, and between the houses I could see clouds gathering in piled-up masses round the horizon. In this part of the world there was only one end to heat like this, and it was going to happen before midnight. My night's run promised to be a stormy one.

The cloud closed over the sky soon after sunset, and from then on it got dark twice as fast as it should have. I was paying my bill to the pretty girl at the desk when I heard the first rumble of thunder very far away in the west. It was a shapeless sound still, but so continuous that I knew that somewhere in that gaunt country I was heading for they were having the father and mother of a thunder-storm. Sooner or later, as I drove west, I should run into it. The unnatural perfection of weather that had so oddly falsified my rediscovery of the world was giving way to something more reassuringly familiar.

It was fully dark when I set out. The first drops of rain struck the windscreen before I had been driving half an hour, and by then the whole sky ahead of me was alive with the intermittent glow of the storm. I climbed a dark winding hill, and as I came over the crest, the wind hit me, almost stopping the car, and the headlights swung down into a long vista of chaos. The windscreen wipers, already running, could hardly clear the glass of the torrent of water thrown against it, and I had a streaky purblind vision of threshing trees and the continuous dance of spray where the rain hit the water swirling on the tarmac. It was more like navigation than driving. I changed into third, even for the run downhill, and found myself ducking my head, as if it was myself, and not the car, that was forcing its way into the storm. Then the whole world turned white round me, and a second later the thunder exploded on the roof.

There was no point in stopping. The lightning, or a falling tree, could catch me just as well stationary as it could moving. But only a fool would try to drive fast in these conditions, and I picked my way through the chaos with a sort of bloody-minded caution. The slope flattened out after a bit, but there were still trees on both sides, with the road flowing like a tormented river between them. The first thing I saw was the red glow of a single reflector on the left-hand margin of the road. Then, as I came up to it, a figure ran out into the glare of the headlights and waved to me. It was a hooded figure. Its clothes flapped about in the wind and shone with the water that poured off it as it stood in the road. I no longer felt as strongly about solitude as I had a couple of days ago, and in any case I had no choice. Performing on that scale, the elemental forces can still put the fear of God into even the most sophisticated man. I should not have liked driving on into the storm if I passed up this appeal for help. I braked cautiously on the streaming tarmac and came to a slithering halt. As I did so, I saw the motor-scooter parked on the roadside grass, with a second figure, equally shrouded and equally wet, standing beside it. I kept the engine turning over and the headlights on.

I leant over and ran the near-side window down. The rain came splashing into it, and a moment later there was a face looking in. It was shrouded in wet plastic from the eyebrows to below the nose, but the nose was long and elegant and the eyes, even in their distress, a little imperious. It was only when she spoke that I knew it was a girl's face. She said, "I'm awfully sorry, but could you possibly get us to Marshcombe? The bloody scooter's broken down."

Marshcombe was no more than fifteen miles ahead and it was not late yet. I could always say I was not going there, but I did not see why I should. I said, "All right. Better get in quick."

She turned and looked over her shoulder without straightening up. She must be a tall girl, because she had to stoop a lot to get her face down to the window. The young man had come forward and was standing behind her. His whole face was uncovered. He had a dark beard full of raindrops, and he looked hesitant and sulky. The girl said, "Come on, it's all right. Get the bags."

He came another step forward and stood there, with the water pouring off him. "What about the bike?" he said.

"Oh, leave the damned thing," she said. "It doesn't work, anyway. No one's going to take it."

The lightning flickered and there was a tremendous bump of thunder, but behind me now, farther up the hill. I sat there in the dry, waiting for the domestic argument to settle itself out there in the wild night. The young man was full of defensive masculine resentment, but there was not much he could say. Even so, he stood there for a moment or two, looking down at the girl as she looked up at him over her shoulder. Then he said, "All right. I'll come back and get her in the morning."

I thought the girl was going to say something, but she had got her way and scorned to have the last word as well. She loosened a draw-string at her neck and with a sudden complicated contortion got her head and arms out of her anorak and pulled off her waterproof trousers. I had a glimpse of a surprisingly long lithe body dressed in something dark and close-fitting, and then the door was flung open and she was in beside me. She shook the wet off her waterproofs, bundled them on to the floor under her legs and shut the door. Then she turned and smiled at me. "Thank you," she said. She was very royal about it. I thought how awful it would be if my car broke down and I found myself in the same trouble as the bearded young man. I did not see why it should, but I was a little apprehensive, all the same.

The rear door was pulled open, and the young man put two small sodden bags on the off-side of the seat. Then he got in himself, waterproofs and all. The girl took a breath but once more thought better of it. She gave me a look which relegated the young man to another world in which neither she nor I had any part. "Right," she said.

I nodded obediently and put the car in gear. Despite my apprehensions, the car moved off when I let the clutch in. No one said anything, but the car was full of steam and the smell of wet clothes and over it all something, a scent or just an emanation, from the warm body beside me. Two miles farther on we ran into clear weather. The sky was full of stars and everything on the ground shone with wet. It was a lovely night, and I was suddenly in no hurry to get to Marshcombe.

When we got there, it was a small huddle of lights in a world of darkness. I stopped the car in the little square, and the young man opened the rear door and began getting himself out. No one had said a word since I had picked them up, and now the silence stretched and snapped with a quiet, decisive violence. The girl said, "I'm not going back. It's your bike."

The young man stopped shuffling in the back of the car. He had one leg out on the pavement. He looked at the back of her head for a moment. "Where are you going, then?" he said.

She turned to me. "Where are you going?"

"Cornwall."

"Can you take me on?"

I had no hesitation now. "I can," I said. I added, "I shall be driving till daylight." I do not quite know why I said that. In some obscure way I suppose I was trying to establish my good faith, with her and even, I think, with the young man. So far as she was concerned, it was quite unnecessary. I did not know about the young man.

She said, "That's fine. Leave my bag, then, will you?"

The young man had nothing to say to her. I had the feeling that everything had been said before I came up with them. He nodded, and got himself and his bag out of the car. He said to me, "Thank you for the ride." Then he shut the rear door, a little too hard for comfort, and turned off into the lamplit square.

She turned to me. "Off we go, then," she said. I looked at her. There was more light here, and I was no longer driving. I wanted to have a good look at her, and I had it. She met my look with a small smile. For herself, she had done all her looking and made up her mind ten miles back. She was dark and, considering that she had come out of a wet anorak, surprisingly neat. She was also friendly, but decisive. I found her extraordinarily easy to get on with.

"Right," I said. I drove on, and for a very long time indeed neither of us said anything. The summer dawn came almost on my right hand as I drove, and suddenly there was more in the world around us than I could see in the headlights. I pulled the car in to the side of the road and turned the headlights off. When I ran my window down, the air outside was dead still and very sweet.

I turned to her. "I generally rest for a bit now," I said, "and do the rest by daylight."

She looked at me very carefully for a moment. Then she nodded. "I'd like that," she said. We got out and stretched our legs on the tarmac. There were trees standing up dark in the fields and behind them a shadowy line of hills. I turned and walked down the road, and the girl walked off in the opposite direction. It was all very easy and matter-of-fact, with no explanations needed. When I came back to the car, she was standing beside it, very tall and slender and absolutely still, watching me come up the dusky road towards her.

She said, "We'll be more comfortable in the back. I've put my bag in front."

She opened the rear door and got in. I got in on the opposite side and sat back in my corner. The seat was slightly damp from the young man's waterproofs, but warm. She moved towards me. I put an arm out, and the next moment her head was on my shoulder. She turned her face up and gave me a quick half-smile. Then she shut her eyes and settled down to sleep, as quick and quiet as a cat. A wave of appalling tenderness flowed over me, so that I thought for a moment I should disturb her by sobbing. But it passed, and was replaced by a sense of peace and security I had not known for God knows how long. I bent down and just touched with my lips the dark top of her head. Then I too shut my eyes. I did not think I should sleep, but did not mind.

In fact I must have slept almost at once. When I woke it was broad daylight, and I knew what Maxwell had said. He had said, "High tide's at—" and mentioned a time. That was where the car came in, because that was why I remembered it. The time was the same as the registration number of my car. I remembered the fact but not the number. Then he had muttered something about getting on, and a moment later he was dead.

33

The girl opened her eyes as suddenly as she had shut them. For a second, as she lifted her head, she stared straight into my eyes with a sort of outraged incredulity. Then she swung away from me and sat up. "Goodness," she said, "I'd forgotten."

CHAPTER 4

I SAID, "But Celia doesn't suit you. You're more like Rosalind. All legs. More than common tall."

"I can't help that. Anyway, Rosalind's fair. Celia's the dark one. The woman low and browner than her brother. I've read the play too, you know. And I'm not all legs."

"All right, of course you're not. I expect I'll get used to it. What are you going to do now?"

"What I was going to do. Have my holiday. Only not with Fred. Fred was a mistake, anyhow. I can't think how I ever thought—". She looked at me, full of indignation, over the remains of the breakfast. "Fred *argued*," she said.

"Yes. Yes, I imagined he might, even from what little I saw of him. I don't imagine that would do."

She said, "It's not— I'm not really the managing sort. I don't expect everyone to agree with me. I'm even prepared on occasion to do what I don't want. But I'm not prepared to be converted about everything. It's too exhausting. What are you going to do?"

"I'm going to buy a boat."

"What sort of a boat? Do you mean a proper boat? With sails?"

"A proper boat with sails. That's if I can find one. I expect I can. There are plenty of them about."

"And then what? Sail it?"

"That's the idea, certainly."

"Here, do you mean?"

"Well—starting from here."

"Do you mean a boat you can cruise on? You must be stinking rich."

"Not in the ordinary way. I've got money saved. I've just come out of prison."

"*Have* you? That's interesting. I've just run away from a convent."

"Have you indeed? You must need your holiday. You found the vows too much for you?"

"It wasn't the vows so much as the Mother Superior. She was just too damned superior."

"What was Fred, then? A lay brother or something?"

"Fred was— Oh, never mind, you started it. All right, you go ahead and buy your boat. And I'll have my holiday."

"Here?" I said.

She looked at me. "Starting from here, anyhow," she said. "But not this hotel. Outside my class. I've got money saved, too, but not that sort of money."

"Where will you stay, then?"

"I'll find somewhere."

Unlike Fred, I did not try to argue. "All right," I said. "It would be nice if we could meet occasionally, all the same. For a drink in the evening, perhaps."

"I'd like that. One of those quaint old water-front bars full of ancient mariners who are stockbrokers all the rest of the year. You know, mermaid frescoes and binnacles for bar-stools."

"All right. Let's go out and find one. In the meantime, may I pay for the breakfast?"

She considered this point perfectly seriously for a moment. Then she said, "Yes. Thank you. It was a good breakfast." We went out to establish our evening rendezvous, and found a pub called the Admiral Howe almost overlooking the boat float. It was of course shut at that time of the morning. From what we could see, it had no binnacles or frescoes, but there were nets with glass floats hung on the walls and coiled ropes in unlikely places. It was near enough.

"Half past six?" I said.

"Seven if the weather holds."

"It will hold all right. All right, seven then. Have a good holiday."

"Buy a nice boat."

We nodded and parted. I did not buy a boat, that day or the next. I had other things to do. I do not know what Celia did, and did not ask. Whatever it was, it made her very brown and somehow sleeker. I looked forward enormously to our evening meeting. We talked about everything under the sun except ourselves, and we hardly so much as touched hands. There was no constraint at all, not at that stage. We were both in a holiday humour, and for me she personified and kept alive the mere pleasure of day-to-day living which I had thought could not last. I did not know what I did for her, except amuse her and buy her the odd drink and meal. I supposed she was seven or eight years younger than I was, but even this I did not know.

When I really set about finding a boat, I wasted very little time. I knew exactly what I wanted, and knew enough not to buy an abject pup. I did not expect to keep her long, and did not mind if I dropped money over her. It was easy, really. I took *Madge* out single-handed on the second afternoon and bought her when I came back in the evening. It seemed an odd, staid name for a boat, but then she was a staid boat. I was not looking for a flyer called *Amaryllis* or *Arctic Tern*. I garaged the car and laid in a few stores while the owner cleared the cheque. Then I took Celia along to see her.

I knew now where I was going, ultimately and by stages. I did not know whether Celia would come with me. I hoped she would, but I counted on nothing. In any case, I was going. I wanted to see if my diamond was negotiable.

We stood at the top of the steps and looked at her. She sat sedately on her moorings, just afloat on the afternoon ebb. Celia said, "So that's her."

"That's her," I said.

"She's not a proud beauty, is she?"

"She's honest."

"What's she got? Inside, I mean."

"Galley next to the cockpit. Two berths and headroom under the coach-house. Loo and wash-house under the forehatch, with the sails. Crouching room only."

"Room for a pipe-cot?"

I looked at her. "Not for a long crew," I said.

She nodded. "Can we get aboard?"

"Yes, yes. There's a pram."

The pram, at the full length of its painter, nestled among a lot of its colleagues at the foot of the steps, sitting on a few inches of dirty water. We went down the steps and I pulled her in cautiously. Celia said, "If we both try to get in here, we'll be on the bottom. And I'm not paddling in that stuff. Let me get in there. She'll just about float me. I'll pick you up somewhere where there's more water."

"Out at the end," I said. "There's another lot of steps."

"You go on," she said. "I'll watch for you." She took the painter from me, gathered it neatly and dropped it into the boat. Then she stepped in and sat down on the centre thwart in one quick neat movement. The boat hardly moved. It was still afloat. She pulled herself out from among the other boats, dropped in the rowlocks, got out the oars and was away before I had moved. I turned and went up the steps. I had seen all I needed. All other considerations apart, she would be a highly competent crew. When I got to the top of the steps, she was sitting out in the clear water, looking up at me.

I said, "Can you cook?"

"Not in half a gale."

"I don't go out in half a gale." I walked along to the end of the arm where the other steps were. There was plenty of water under them. Celia brought the pram in as I came down the steps. "Why didn't you tell me you were an expert?" I said.

"I didn't think it was relevant." She put the stern in to the steps and I got in. When we got on board, she went all over *Madge*, looking at things and saying nothing. I sat in the cockpit and waited. She did not want me to show her round. When she had finished, she came back and sat down opposite me. "She's all right," she said.

"I'm glad you like her."

"But you're right about the fo'c'sle."

"Yes."

For a bit neither of us said anything. The sunlight lay placidly on the flat water and the piled-up town all round it. As usual, she was thinking, and I knew better than to interrupt. Finally she said, "It's up to you, I think."

"On the contrary," I said, "it's up to you."

"Oh, I'd like to come. But only on conditions. It's you that's got to sign on, not me."

"I'll sign," I said. "If it doesn't work, I'll just have to put you ashore somewhere."

We looked at each other. I should not like to say what I was really thinking. I just did not want to leave her behind.

"All right," she said. "When do we sail?"

"I should say tomorrow. You'll want to check stores and do some shopping."

"That's right. And where do we sail?"

"Eastwards. Strictly coastal stuff, at least until we know a lot more about her."

"I agree. Now let me have a proper look at what you've got."

Our meeting at the Admiral Howe that evening was different from any of our earlier meetings. It was not only that we now had practical matters of common interest to discuss. There was that, too, of course, but there was not only that. In an odd sort of way, it was like a farewell meeting. Whatever happened next, the old relation was coming to an end, and it had been a very good one. There was the possibility, which we both saw, that we were killing it for the sake of something which might be better, but might equally turn out to be disastrous. We watched each other, for the first time, with a touch of unwilling but unavoidable calculation. It was rather like buying a house and settling down in a place where up to now you have spent only pleasant holidays. You may be putting your pleasure on a permanent footing, but you may also be uncovering the snags.

These were never late sessions, and now we got up to go long before closing time. When we got outside, we walked in silence to the edge of the quay and stood there, looking out over the float. The tide was in and the gleaming motionless water brimmed the dark walls. Celia put into words what was in both our minds. "I hope it's going to be all right," she said.

"I'm sure it's worth trying, anyhow."

"Yes. Yes, of course it is. All right, I'll be down, bag and baggage, for the morning tide. Say about ten?"

"Ten will be fine," I said. "How long have you got?"

"Altogether? About a week."

I nodded. "A week should kill or cure," I said.

"I don't want anything killed or cured. But let's hope for the best. Good night, Peter."

"Good night, Celia."

She went off in her long neat stride between the lighted windows and the shadowy water. I watched her for a moment and then went back to my hotel. I had some working out to do. What I had to work out was whether a week would or would not take *Madge* to Leremouth. Leremouth was where I was going, and I had not yet quite made up my mind whether I wanted to go there in Celia's company.

I was going to Leremouth because I was reasonably certain that that was where Evan Maxwell had been going when I stopped him. The calculation had not been particularly difficult, but it seemed to me convincing. I had telephoned my insurance brokers for the missing car number. It was 952. The letters of course did not matter. High tide, the particular high tide Maxwell had had so much in mind, had been at 9:52. I had stopped him in full career at about eight in the evening. It had been late June and broad daylight. He was a thrusting driver, but the roads in those parts did not allow a high average. Assuming that he would want a bit of time in hand when he got there, I reckoned that his destination could not be more than fifty miles away, and he was still more than forty miles from the nearest point of sea. I laid an arc on a fifty-mile radius from where the thing had happened, and found that it took in a very limited stretch of coast. Not only was it limited in extent; it was by south-coast standards fairly empty. There were only half a dozen places on it which would rate a mention in the local tide tables, and if a man like Maxwell thought high tide at any place was at 9:52, it would be because he had got the figure from a table. All I wanted was the local tide tables for that 17th of June four years ago. If they showed a high tide at about the right time of the evening. I was on the right lines. If they gave 9:52 for high water at a particular place, then that was the place I wanted.

On the second day of Celia's holiday I had driven to Tanchester and got out the back file of the *Tanchester Chronicle.* It was there, straight away. Leremouth 9:52. I had never been to Leremouth, and was certainly not going there then, but on the map it looked promising. The Lere ran out in a long tidal estuary, and in places like that the tides take on an exaggerated importance. There, for what it was worth, was my diamond. That was what Mr. Matthews wanted to know; and now I knew it and he did not. Whether it was worth much to me I could not guess, but I intended to find out. If I could make nothing of it myself, it was almost certainly a thing which Mr. Matthews would be ready in some form to pay for. But the thing was not impossible. Leremouth was a small place, and I had a date and a time, even if it was some time ago. Something had been due to happen, and presumably had happened, when the floodtide came to the full on that June evening four years ago, something that was important enough to bring Evan Maxwell hurtling down-country in his big car without telling his friends where he was going. If I went to Leremouth, I might, even now, be able to find out what it was.

And now I was very well placed to go. Mr. Matthews was expecting me to cruise, and I was going to. I should be coasting, calling at plenty of places before I got to Leremouth. Who, even observing my movements with the utmost suspicion, was to distinguish my call there from any of the others? In the meantime, there was Celia, who might or might not leave the ship before we got there. If it seemed better, as it might still be, that I should go to Leremouth by myself, it would be easy enough to delay my arrival until after she had left. The whole thing was full of uncertainties and imponderables, and I regarded them all with equal pleasure. At this stage I could not see any chance of trouble anywhere—except, of course, in the sea, but that was always there and was part of the pleasure. I went to bed in a state of placid contentment which had by now become almost a habit of mind; and the weather, set fair in sympathy, brought up another perfect day of yellow sunlight and the light southerly breeze which would take me where I wanted to go at the sort of speed I wanted to go at with the minimum of effort and adventure. I paid my hotel bill with a proper sense of gratitude, and was waiting for Celia when she came to the top of the steps, characteristically, at exactly ten.

We cast off our moorings and motored gently out between the pier heads with the pram on a long tow astern. A dozen people watched us go. Patient pier-head fishermen, up-country people on holiday, the small perennial population of land-bound sea-watchers that a place like this always provides. They watched us with the half-envious interest with which anyone in his right mind watches any ship put to sea. For all I knew, there might be one person among them who had come down for the sole purpose of seeing us go, and who would hurry back to the nearest telephone to report our departure and the course we set once we got outside. If so, the best of luck to him. I looked up at the motionless intermittent faces as we went slowly past them, but I did not know which of them it might be, or if there was any such person there at all.

I cut the engine and for a time we stood out south-southwest, as near the mild wind as she would reasonably sail, until the land lay behind us in a patchwork of greens and browns, and the only thing that mattered was the green water under us and the blue emptiness all round. Then I let out more sail and turned *Madge* due east across the wind, pointing for the blue distant outline of Carristowe Head. All this time Celia had been spreadeagled on the foredeck, full of the serene professional idleness of the expert who knows there is absolutely nothing that needs doing. Now she got up and came aft down the weather side of the ship, very long and easy-moving and completely at home. "What about coffee?" she said. "Too late?"

"Never too late," I said. "Coffee, please."

CHAPTER 5

THAT FIRST NIGHT the wind was so fair and the weather so kind that we decided to keep sailing and take alternate four-hour watches. There was also, perhaps, the idea in both our minds that this postponed a problem which might be more easily settled when we had been a little longer at sea. I had seen enough of Celia's handling of the boat to know that I could leave her at the tiller, especially in conditions like these, and get my sleep below with an easy mind. We hove to for a short time, drifting in gently towards the land, while we dined in some state on Celia's cooking. Then she took over, heading a bit more into the wind to make up our leeway, while I washed up and got out blankets and sleeping bags and rigged the lights. At about nine I came up and sat beside her in the cockpit.

The whole world was awash with a huge saffron glow, and the land, already shadowy and dotted with lights, lay comfortably along the lee sky. We said very little, and that hardly above a whisper, as if the silence was too good to spoil. Like the able seaman she was, she hardly took her eyes off the Carristowe light winking just over the port bow. I watched that delicate, incisive profile, with the dark hair blowing gently round it, wondering what was going on in her mind. At ten I said, "All right. I'll take her now. You go below and get some sleep. I'll call you at two."

She nodded and moved over while I took over the tiller and

settled myself comfortably. Then she stood up, very straight and supple against the gentle swinging of the boat. I knew that she was looking at me now, watching me as she had that first night in the car. I looked up at her for a moment, smiling, but she had no smile to answer mine. She was solemn and intent, as if I was something to be observed and steered by, like the Carristowe light. I looked ahead again, but still she did not move. At last she let her breath go and turned towards the hatch. I thought she had been going to say something, but had thought better of it. At any rate, I thought that whatever had been in her mind, she had settled it one way or the other. She went down into the hatch and then turned, with only her head and shoulders showing. "Good night, Peter," she said.

I said, "Good night, dear Celia," without taking my eyes off the Carristowe light. Then she went below, and I was left with only the boat and the sea, wondering more than ever what would come of it.

For a very long time nothing came of it at all. Against the pattern of the ship the stars moved very slowly overhead, and the fixed lights on shore crept westwards almost as slowly. Only the Pole Star and the light ahead stayed where they were, the one because that was in the nature of things and the other because I held it there. Mr. Matthews and Evan Maxwell and whatever had happened at Leremouth four years ago seemed very remote and infinitesimally important. I did not want to go down and make love to Celia in the cabin, or to have her come up to me. For her to sleep and for me to steer seemed as good a way as any of seeing time out. Like Browning's man doing his last ride with his mistress, I could have believed that the thing could be fixed so and ever so abide, and would have settled for it if it could.

But the stars moved and time went, and good discipline is of the essence of sailing. When it was just on two, I lashed the tiller, slid the hatch cover very quietly forward and went down into the dark cabin. I could just hear the movement of the water along the sides of the ship and every now and then the minute, friendly noises of wood or cordage yielding to changing stresses which are one of the joys of sailing a ship on a mild sea. I also heard, straining my ears, the gentle regular sound of a human machine ticking over in neutral. I switched on one of the small electric lights in the cabin top and looked at her.

She lay on her back, chin up, mouth firmly shut, dark lashes flat on her cheek. She was tidy and composed even in her sleep. I stooped until my face was directly over hers and stayed there, unwilling to wake her and fascinated, as any thinking man must be, by the mystery of sleep. I do not know how long this lasted, but suddenly her eyes were wide open and staring straight up into mine. The world went dark in a moment, because the eyes had nothing in them but terror.

It did not last. Her quick mind took control, and I suppose, too, she saw the answering distress in my face looking down at hers. She turned her head sideways, as if to cut off the line of too vivid communication between us, and at the same time I straightened up and stood back from her. I said, "Celia! Celia, it's two. Your watch." I said it exactly as I should have said it if I had merely called her from the hatch and had not seen what I had seen. Nothing could change the fact that I had seen it, and I did not think anything would ever be the same now that I had, but above all the thing must not be acknowledged. She rolled over and sat up in her sleeping bag, ruffling through her hair with her hands and blinking in the light. It was all perfectly natural, and the quick half-smile that followed it was Celia to the life. But it was an act. Some people, women particularly, go almost continuously from one act to another, and there is no harm in it, because putting on an act is simply their normal way of conducting personal relations. But it was not Celia's way, and the act, perfectly natural as it was, stuck out like a piece of ham business on a lit stage.

She said, "Oh— Sorry, I was sleeping like the dead. All right. Give me a couple of minutes and I'll be up."

I nodded and went back up into the cockpit, leaving the light on in the cabin. *Madge* had wandered slightly under her lashed helm, and I put her back on course, holding the tiller a little stiffly. The night air struck cold after the warmth below, and I shivered suddenly with an odd confusion of mental and physical distress. Celia put her head out of the hatch and said, "Would you like a drink or anything before you turn in?"

"I don't think so," I said. "It might keep me awake. What about you?"

"Not for me, thanks." She came up into the cockpit, well muffled to keep in the warmth she had brought from sleep. She turned and looked at our course. "Keep on as we're going?" she said.

"Just as we're going. Give us plenty of sea room round the head. It'll be light before your watch is up. Sing out if anything worries you, or if you're getting cold. I don't need all that sleep."

"I'll be all right," she said. She took the tiller from me and settled herself to steer. I went down into the cabin, pulling the hatch cover back over me. It was warm and quiet down below, and the cabin smelt of Celia. I did what I had to do, put the light out and crawled into my sleeping bag. Then I lay on my back, with my hands behind my head, staring up into the darkness. I had never felt less like sleep in my life.

Fright was unlike Celia, as unlike her as the act of sleepy confusion which had followed it. It was true she had been deep asleep, and it is possible to wake up frightened, even if the thing that awakens you is not frightening in itself. But I did not think this was what had happened. I thought she had woken up with the light, and seen me stooping over her, and been frightened by what she saw. I had had nothing in my mind, and could have had nothing in my face, but a cautious affection for the girl herself and the slightly awe-stricken fascination of the waking observer for the mere image of sleep. But she could hardly have looked more frightened if I had come below with Tarquin's ravishing stride and put my hand on her bare breast. I had to ask myself what there was in me to frighten her, and I did not at all like any of the possible answers. Odd as it seemed to me, I was, I supposed, publicly branded as a man of violence. A very dangerous man, Mr. Matthews had said. But I had not told her this. I should not have minded telling her. I had told her I had just come out of jail, and she had brushed it aside with nonsense. I had assumed she did not believe me, and because I knew she was in no danger from me, I had not gone on with it. I supposed the thing might nevertheless have stuck in her mind and left her worrying about it. If so, the sooner it was cleared up, the better.

I started to climb out of my sleeping bag, determined to go up and have it out with her there and then. But another possibility, much more unpalatable, stopped me. I had to face the fact that she might already know about me and what I had done; and she could know this only if someone, Mr. Matthews or someone, had told her. She was already an intrinsic, almost a necessary, part of my contentment and freedom. Nevertheless, she might herself be part of this dark business I had got myself mixed up in and had decided, like a fool, to go further into. If she knew more about it than I did, it might be the thing itself, and not only me, that frightened her. I pulled the sleeping bag round my neck and rolled over on my side. There was nothing I could do about it, after all. Only watch her, and try to make up my mind. But my peace was gone. It had perished irretrievably in that split second when I had looked into her eyes between sleeping and waking, and nothing would bring it back. And down inside me, in the dingy kennel where it slept, my anger stirred at the inescapable possibility that I had been made a fool of.

I slept, of course, after that. The mere physical conditions made it next to impossible not to, and God knows I had no wish to stay awake. When I woke, there was grey daylight outside the scuttles, and it was nearly half past five. What had happened those few hours earlier, before I went to sleep, was very clear in my mind, but seemed very remote. I have never been able to understand the warning not to let the sun go down on your wrath. It seems to me much the best thing to do with it. One of the great things about sleep is its ability to leave the judgment unimpaired but to take the heat out of your emotional reaction to it. It was still a different Celia sitting up there in the cockpit, but I was already on terms with her.

I pulled myself out of my bag and got my feet on the floor. The boat was still sailing as she had, lying slightly over on her port side and rocking very gently as the southerly swell went under her. I got up and looked out of the portside scuttle. There was the head, standing up dark and grey against the paler grey of the sky, and a comfortable distance down-wind. In her placid way, *Madge* had made reasonable speed, and there was nothing wrong with our course. The alarms of the night seemed smaller than ever against the solid advantages of a competent crew. I dressed myself and put the kettle on. Then I slid back the hatch and put my head out. It was about ten to six.

Celia, curled up on the bench with the tiller under her arm, moved nothing but her eyes, and for a moment we looked at each other in the clear white light of morning. Then I smiled and she smiled back. I said, "Good morning. All well?"

She stretched and lowered her feet into the well of the cockpit. "All well," she said.

"Getting cold?"

"A bit, but it's a honey of a morning."

"The kettle's on," I said. "Tea or coffee? And will you make it or shall I?"

"I will, if you'll come and take her. Tea for me, I think, at this hour. You too?"

"Please." I climbed out of the hatch, surprised but elated, as you never fail to be, by the sheer chilly beauty of the morning air. "No trouble in the night?" I said.

She moved over and I took the tiller from her. "No trouble that I know of," she said.

I settled for that, and was glad to. "Good," I said. "You get the tea, then."

The wind fell away as the day advanced, though what there was of it stayed southerly. By the time we had fully cleared the head and were ready to stand in northwards, it had practically gone altogether. The mainsail, left to itself, hung out limply over the side of the boat, and the foresail gave up completely. We lolloped in slowly on the oily swell, hardly knowing whether it was the wind or the sea that carried us. But time meant very little to us, and after a night's sailing we were content to leave things as they were. We got the sails down finally when we were just outside Carristowe harbour, and motored in to find ourselves a mooring. By the time we had got straightened up it was well into the afternoon.

Celia said she had shopping to do. I said I would come ashore with her, have a swim somewhere away from the harbour and meet her later for a drink. I pulled in the pram while she went below to make those ritual preparations without which a woman cannot go shopping even off a boat like *Madge* in a town like Carristowe. When she came up, she was looking mysteriously but unmistakably smarter, though I could not see what she had done to herself. She stood in the cockpit, looking out through the harbour mouth to the shining blank of the Channel stretching away southwards. She said, "It's going to take you an awful long time to get anywhere in these conditions."

"I'm not trying to get anywhere," I said. "What about you?"

"Me? I'm just saving my fare home. I'm not going to save much, by the look of it. Where'll we be in a week's time?"

"How the devil do I know? Devon somewhere, if you want me to hazard a guess."

"There's an awful lot of Devon."

"There is, in fact. That's what makes it so likely that we shall be there. But the natives are friendly, wherever I have to put you ashore. Does it worry you?"

"I don't expect so." She climbed down into the pram and settled herself on the rowing thwart. "Any more for the shore?" she said.

"Wait while I get my things." When I came up, I said, "Shall we dine ashore? Save you cooking on board."

"As you like. Or I can get something to cook."

"Cook's day off. Let's go on the town. There must be somewhere."

She looked at Carristowe across the harbour. She said, "Can you dine on fish-and-chips and candy floss?"

"It can't be that bad. If it is, you buy something to eat aboard. I leave it to you."

She nodded. "Let's go, then."

When we were up on the quay, she said, "Rendezvous where and when?"

"Here, I should think. Then we can decide what to do. How long do you want?"

"Probably less than you, if you're going to swim away from the drains. About an hour?"

"All right. Say six. The shops will be shut and the pubs open."

She went off very purposefully towards the shopping streets, such as they were. I walked across to the other side of the harbour, found myself cut off by the sharp fall of the cliff and turned back into the town, looking for the nearest way out between the houses. I took the first street to the right, but it jinked left again, leading in towards the middle of the town. I saw the telephone box as soon as I turned out into the next street. I was quite close to it before I saw who was in it. She had her back to me and could not have seen me.

I stopped at once. There was no conceivable reason why Celia should not want to telephone someone as soon as she got ashore. She might have parents, she must have someone, interested in where she was and liable to worry if they did not hear. Nevertheless, I stopped and turned back between the houses, looking for another way out of the town. I found a place to swim at the bottom of the cliff, before the land fell away into the regular bathing beaches. It was utterly quiet, and you could go in anywhere in these conditions. I came out of the water and sat naked in the late sun, feeling the salt crystallize on my skin, but lacking the peace of mind necessary to a proper enjoyment. I was back in the town well before the hour was up.

This time I went straight down the High Street towards the harbour. I thought I might see Celia somewhere and not have to wait for her on the quay. The car pulled out from the kerb about twenty-five yards in front of me and then turned off into a side street before it reached me. I noticed it because it did not look the sort of car anyone would drive round a small sea-side town in the holiday season and that golden weather. It was too dark and shut up. Also it seemed in a hurry. I did not notice the number or the driver. As I came along the pavement, I saw Celia standing looking into a shop window. She was standing just at the place the car had pulled away from. She had two carrier bags full of parcels. The shop she was looking into was a toy shop. Before I got to her, she turned and went off along the pavement ahead of me, making towards the harbour. I came up with her and said, "Carry your bags, Miss?"

"Oh, hullo," she said. "Good swim? You've been quick."

"A good swim, thank you. Why the toys?"

"Toys?"

"You were looking in a toy shop. Shall I buy you a teddy bear?"

"Oh, that. No, thank you. I have a nephew and a conscience."

"I see. I thought you looked lost in thought. What about dinner?"

"Nothing much here. Only one likely hotel, and they're very early. I've bought some steak."

"Home, then. Have we anything to drink with it?"

"Only beer on board. I thought I'd better ask."

"Wise girl. You go on down to the boat. I'll get something."

I bought a bottle of Burgundy at an off-licence and joined her at the top of the steps. There was not a breath of wind now. *Madge* was mirrored in detail on the glassy water under her. A painted ship upon a painted ocean. The wash of the pram stirred the surface and threw little wave-lines of light along her topsides and under her counter, but when we got aboard and pushed the pram out to the end of its painter, the water settled down again like oil. The paintwork of the coach-house was hot in the sun, but it was surprisingly cool down below in the cabin, and quiet after the noise of the town.

We drank gin and hung the wine above the Calor gas stove, so that it would warm up while Celia cooked the steak. It was a good meal. I drank two glasses of wine to Celia's one. We cleared the dishes away into the galley and folded up the table, and I looked at her, sitting on her berth opposite me in the faint golden light that came in through the scuttles. "Tell me about your nephew," I said.

She got up and stood there, looking down at me. She said, "I don't think you're interested in my nephew."

"Only in his existence," I said. "Not the details, however lucid and convincing. Only in what makes you stand in front of a particular shop."

She said, "I don't know what you mean," and I reached out and caught her round the waist. She did not try to pull away. She held herself absolutely rigid, looking down at me as I looked up at her. "You're breaking the rules," she said.

I said, "To hell with the rules. The whole damned agreement is null and void. Void for misrepresentation, or something. I'm a fool, dear Celia, but not all that of a fool."

She said again, "I don't know what you mean." Then she tried to break away from me towards the hatch. She tried very suddenly, but I held her, and she bent over quickly and bit one of my hands. After that it was all in. She never screamed, though in that small harbour someone would have heard her. She fought silently as long as there was anything to fight for, but when the fight had gone out of both of us, she turned her head away and I thought she was crying.

I kissed the dark hair over her ear and pulled a blanket over us. Later, much later, I felt her rouse herself and go back to her own berth. I let her go. When I woke, it was quite dark, and my watch said nearly half past one. I could see the square of sky full of stars above the open hatch, but the cabin was in pitch darkness. I switched on a light and looked across at the other berth. It was empty. I went up into the cockpit. The pram had gone, too. The galley was full of greasy dishes and empty glasses. The cabin, when I went down into it, was chilly from the open hatch, but still smelt faintly of what had happened there. I slammed the hatch shut, took off what few clothes I still had on and crawled into my sleeping bag. When it was light, I would clean up and swim after the pram. For the moment sleep was the thing, and I slept.

CHAPTER 6

I DREAMED that Celia was up there in the cockpit, steering the ship. I got up and put my head out of the hatch and we looked at each other. I said, "All well?" and she said, "All well." Then I began to wake up a bit. I still felt that the ship was under way. There was a movement which penetrated my receding sleep. But I knew by now that all was not well. When I was fully awake, I found *Madge* rocking gently but steadily on her moorings and Celia and the pram gone. I got up and looked out, not into the cockpit, but through the scuttle over my berth.

The weather had changed. The sky was heavily clouded, and there was enough wind blowing in from the sea to rock the boat where she lay. It was dark and rather stuffy in the cabin and would be cold outside. I set about washing and dressing, but remembered that I had to swim ashore at some point. I put on my swimming trunks, still slightly damp from the day before, and a guernsey on my top half, and went up into the cockpit. It was blowing, not hard but steadily, from the southeast, and the air, as I had expected, was chilly. I looked over to the quayside steps. The pram was there, right enough. I went back into the cabin and looked round. I wondered if she had left a note or something, but there was nothing at all. All her things were gone. There was a mark of her dark pink lipstick on one of the gin glasses. I put it aside from the rest of the washing up. Then I took my guernsey off and, without giving myself too long to think about it, went head first over the side.

I had expected the water to be cold and it was, but I think it did me good. To have to swim after the pram roused my fading antagonism and made me a little angry again. I said to myself, "God damn the little bitch, she could have asked." But more than half my anger was against myself, because I had slept through it all and let her go away without explanations and with no means of tracing her. When I reached the quay, I climbed out on the steps. The pram was in perfect order, on enough painter to allow for any amount of tide, with the rowlocks in-board and the oars carefully stowed under the thwarts. This did not make me feel any better about it. There was no note here either, nothing at all. She must have gone up the steps some time in the small hours and walked into the town carrying her bag. I wondered, a bit savagely, if she had gone straight to the call-box, and if the dark closed car had come along and picked her up. But I did not really know, and now I never should. The wind struck cold as I stood wet on the steps. I untied the painter, got out the rowlocks and oars and paddled back to the ship. This time I did wash and dress myself. Then I washed up everything but the gin glass. I rinsed the gin out of that and put it back in the locker as it was.

I went up and looked at the weather again, and later got the weather report on the radio. There was nothing special to worry about. The shift in the wind might slow down my progress east-wards, but that did not matter, because it did not matter, so far as I knew, when I got to Leremouth. The great thing was to keep going. It was not the sort of weather to lie up in, and in any case I did not want to stay in Carristowe. I had to take *Madge* with me, but at least I could get away from the harbour and the telephone box and toy shop.

I pulled the pram on board and lashed it on the coach-house, not because I expected trouble with it, but because it might slow me up and because if I was going to be single-handed, it would be one thing less to think about. By ten I was all set to go. I got sail up, slipped my moorings and motored straight out into the wind. When I was well clear, I cut the engine, sheeted in and pointed *Madge* almost due south on a port tack. I reckoned that when I went about, I could reach pretty well across the wind and make enough speed to bring me in to one of several reasonably snug moorings well before dark. I was not going to do any night sailing single-handed. It was not that sort of trip.

All the same, I was glad of a certain amount of work to do. To have the boat sloshing into the wind and knocking up a bit of water gave me the same sort of relief as I had got from my early-morning swim. Something that had meant far too much to me was over, and I did not want too much time to think about it. I headed out to sea, conscious all the time of a nagging disquiet and I suppose hoping, if I went far and fast enough, to get away from it.

The weather got worse, gradually but unmistakably, all that week. Until the last day I was never in any sort of trouble, or even in apprehension of trouble, but I had to plan my moves more and more carefully, and all the time the sailing got more adventurous and tiring. My admiration for *Madge* grew steadily. There was a strategic consideration here which I did not overlook. After a series of short hauls and one-night stands all the way up the coast, I wanted to stay at Leremouth for a bit when I got there. To get there after a rough sail and with nasty conditions brewing outside would provide the best possible reason for lying up for a bit. I did not know if my progress from Carristowe had been watched, but I had to assume it had.

By the evening of the sixth day I was lying in Storridge Bay, with nothing much more than Bonnet Point between me and the Lere estuary. It was blowing southwest now, and the sea was starting to get up under a dark sky. So long as I could get round Bonnet next day, the thing was timing itself perfectly, but I thought it might be a bumpy ride. I was right. I got away as soon as it was light, and had to thrash my way out in a series of short tacks. I had to get well out, so that, if anything did go wrong, my leeway would carry me clear round the point and not into the shambles at its foot. The further out I got, the wetter and bumpier things were, and the temptation to turn off the wind too soon was very strong. I kept at it until early in the afternoon. Then I went for the last time on to the starboard tack and eased her gradually off the wind. She went sloshing off, rolling alarmingly at times in the beam sea, but making reassuring progress across the line of the point. I was not going to risk a gybe in these conditions, but when I was finally and unmistakably to leeward of the point, I pointed her nearer the wind again and sheeted in. She made a fuss about it and took a bit of water as she put her nose into the sea, but she was a stout-hearted boat and gradually got more way on her. As soon as I could I went about and then, safely on a port tack, let her off across the wind again, and fairly scurrried for the shelter of the point.

I had had all the sailing I wanted for the moment. I crouched there in the cockpit, with one foot braced on the opposite bench and my back turned to the wind and sea, looking up over my shoulder every now and then at the great black cliffs on the lee side of Bonnet. Gradually we crept under them, and gradually the sea settled and lost its menace. Under the point here the wind came almost southerly, and I let the mainsheet go until we were pretty well running in with the wind under our port quarter. I could see the houses of Leremouth grouped on the western side of the channel, and was beginning to look for the harbour entrance, when the fore halyard parted, and the foresail ballooned out for a moment and then went over the side. Coming when it did, this was not disaster. The boat did need her headsail now, and once I was sure that the sheets were holding and that the sail would not be lost, I left it as it was, rather than leave tiller and mainsheet and risk a gybe while I tried to sort it out. But I did not like to think what this would have meant if it had happened several hours earlier, when I was still making out into the wind on the wrong side of the point. The possibility that I was being watched meant nothing to me now. All I wanted was to get *Madge* inside that harbour and firmly moored.

It was a dark afternoon and raining steadily. The estuary was high and steep on its western side, where the town was, and flat and low-lying on the east. The whole effect, under that weeping sky, was sombre and rather dreary. Leremouth was port after stormy seas, and as that I was glad to see it, but I did not take to it. It sat uneasily on the steep flank of Bonnet, crouching a bit under the hanging woods that grew above and inland of it, and staring out across the sands of the estuary at the flats on the far side. I could not, from here, see it as a holiday resort, though I supposed it must do some business that way.

I could see the entrance now. Inside the river here there was no more than a steady breeze behind the boat and plenty of sea room. I sheeted in a bit and swung her right round into the wind. Then I let everything go and ran forward to get the mainsail down. I dragged the sodden foresail on board in case there was enough halyard left on it to foul the screw, and then went below and started the engine. All this time we drifted gently stern first into the river, but there was plenty of room and no particular hurry. A quarter of an hour later I chugged in slowly between the harbour heads. There were the usual people watching, even at that time of day and in that weather. I looked at them all carefully in turn as I came in under them. I do not know what I expected to see. There was a stagnant smell in the air, as if the harbour water was never properly changed. I got the boat moored, had one more look round Leremouth, thought no more of it than I had the first time, and went below to make tea and get myself dry.

For the moment all I wanted was physical comfort and nothing to worry about. I managed that very quickly. It was not really cold outside, only wet and blustery, and below-decks on a boat the size of *Madge* can be one of the snuggest places on earth. Mentally I was tired, but no more than after a long car journey in difficult conditions. I drank hot tea with whisky in it, basked in the warmth of the gas stove and enjoyed the mere stillness and security of the boat. This did not last. I got up and looked out of the scuttles at Leremouth. It was going to get dark early, and already there were lights about. Somewhere out there there might be someone watching me, and from now on I was acting a part. Up to now I had done only what I should have done anyhow if I had never met Mr. Matthews at Burton St. Michael. There had been no need to falsify anything. Now I had come to Leremouth at the end of a journey and with a purpose in my mind, only nothing I did must be allowed to make the difference apparent. The enemy had nothing to do with Leremouth. They were as much outsiders there as I was. In fact, of course, Leremouth was common ground of equal interest to both the enemy and myself. The difference was that I knew this and they did not.

I took my head away from the scuttle and sat down again on my berth. What I was really concerned with was Celia. I am no better at sorting out my motives than most people, but it did not need any special honesty or perspicacity to know that. I wanted to know where she came into the thing, if she came into it at all. For more than one reason, I hoped she did. Now that she had gone, I missed her very much. I opened the hatch and put my head out. It had stopped raining. The sky was still clouded, but there was a mild air blowing fitfully about the harbour. For all I knew, the sea was still driving hard on to the broken rocks at the foot of Bonnet Point, but it was difficult to believe in it here. It all seemed a long way away and a long time ago. I unlashed the pram from the top of the coach-house and let it down into the water. Then I went below and put on my shore-going clothes. I was no longer tired and had too little to occupy my mind. I thought I would go and have a closer look at Leremouth.

There was not much of it, less even than there was of Carristowe. A small fishing harbour, which might or might not have a few fishermen left, a couple of streets of shops, a few more streets of small houses, one road climbing up through the woods and another running back along the side of the estuary, and the estuary itself. And two pubs. There was not much to choose between them, but I picked the better lit of the two. I did not even notice its name.

Pretty well everyone in the place turned and looked at me as I came in. There was no mistaking the look. These were locals. There was not, in fact, much holiday business in Leremouth, or if there was, it went to the other house. They were all perfectly friendly. They did not, once they had had a look at me, mind my joining the party, but it was a party and for me it was joining it or nothing. I joined it. They all said good evening in a variety of local voices, and I said good evening and ordered myself a double whisky, because that was what I had started the evening on over my tea. There was a stool to spare and I sat on it. They were all on stools, even the landlord on his side of the bar.

A genial face at the other end of the bar said, "You're off that sloop that came in this evening—*Madge*, isn't it?" The geniality had a pretty heavy veneer of alcohol, but it was genuine. He would be the soul of geniality, drunk or sober. He had a middle-class voice, which the others had not. He also had a small moustache and a tailor-made tweed jacket. The whole effect was slightly raffish but, as I say, genial.

"That's right," I said.

"I watched you come round the point," he said. Just for a moment my mind stiffened, but this was nonsense. It was not a local I was looking for. Or, I thought, anyone who did not mind admitting he had been watching me. "I wondered if you'd be all right, but you seemed to be coping. You on your own? You were sailing single-handed."

"On my own, yes. She doesn't take much handling. Did you see me lose my foresail?"

He showed elaborate concern. I think he really felt it in a slightly clouded sort of way. "No," he said. "Did you do that?"

"Only when I was inside the river. Or under the point, anyway."

He laughed cheerfully. "Well, thank God for that," he said. "I only watched you round the point. When I saw you were clear, I lost interest. Then I saw you on your moorings just now and recognised you. The boat, I mean, of course. Drink that up and have another one. You be staying here long?"

I had no answer to that, but I thought to myself, show willing. It is where the natives are friendly that you decide to stay the night. "Well," I said, "I've no fixed plans, really. I must confess, I was beginning to feel I'd done enough sailing for a bit."

"Well, you drop your hook here for a bit. Might do worse. We can do with a new face."

I said to the landlord, "Not many visitors? I should have thought there would be."

He said, "Well—" It was a long-drawn-out syllable, and it said a lot. "I'd say we don't cater for them, really. We get a few, of course. But there isn't much for them to do."

A man half-way along the bar said, "No sands, that's what it is. It's sands they want."

"Not in the river?" I said, and the genial man laughed.

"Whisky for you?" he said. "Bert, give my friend a nice whisky. And another for me, too. Plenty of sand in the river," he said. "You must have seen. But not the sort of sand you play about on."

"What is it? Dangerous?" I said.

"Well, it's that too in places. You want to know it. But mainly it's the tide. Nips up and down a bit. All sand one moment and all water the next. You're all right in the harbour." He was anxious to reassure me, and once more the anxiety was genuine. "You won't find yourself on the bottom in the night. But once you get up-river a bit, it's very flat and very shallow. There's a channel, of course, where the land water comes down. But that's not much. The rest's all flats."

I nodded. "Sounds interesting," I said. "I'll explore some time. But no good for holiday-makers, I can see that."

The genial man seemed to brood on what I had said. Then he suddenly lit up. "You're not interested in birds?" he said. He waited, almost breathlessly, for my reply. But he saw in my face what was coming, and the light went out of his.

"Not really," I said. "I mean—I like seeing them around. I know most of the ordinary ones. But I'm not an expert, I'm afraid."

He nodded. "Pity," he said. "We've got some interesting ones here. On the river, you see, and on the marshes higher up."

I drank his double whisky on top of my own, and my heart warmed to him. "You must show me," I said.

"Really?" He looked at me as if I was humouring him, as of course I was. He was not wholly satisfied. "Well, we'll see," he said.

Later, when we got outside in the rather chilly darkness, he said, "I tell you what. You must come up and see us. We're up on top of the point. My wife would be glad to see you. I told you, we don't get many visitors. Will you do that?"

"I'd like it very much."

"Good, good. I must be off now, or I'll catch it. But you'll be here for a few days, anyhow. I'll come down and see you tomorrow, and we'll fix things up. That be all right?"

"That will be fine," I said. "If the pram's alongside and you don't see me on deck, give me a hail. But I've got to get that damned foresail up some time."

"I know," he said. "Climb the mast and all that. But there's no hurry if you're not sailing at once."

"That's true," I said. We parted with tremendous cordiality. I really rather liked him. I still did not know his name, and I wondered about his wife, from whom, presumably, he was going to catch it if he was late. I did not necessarily believe this. It is a familiar gambit, this pretence of domestic tyranny, though wives do it more than husbands. I suppose to gain sympathy. I must fly, darling, or George will be simply furious. And then half the time George turns out to be a small man with spectacles and no fury in him. The genial man could be pretty irritating, of course, but I liked him nevertheless.

But when I got back on board, what I really thought about was the tide. The tide that nipped up and down a bit, transforming a whole small world, all sand one minute, all water the next. Up-river, up between the marshes and the sand flats, there would be places where the tide meant everything. I should have, as I had said, to explore.

Meanwhile, the natives were friendly and I had every excuse to stay. I ate a quick meal out of a tin, got into my sleeping bag and slept like the dead.

CHAPTER 7

IT WAS a wonderful position for a house, provided it was the sort of thing you liked. It would not be to everyone's taste. I did not think Mr. Tomlinson could have built it for himself. He was not much older than I was, which was not old enough. It would have been built in the late twenties or early thirties. It was the kind of thing they were building then in this kind of position. A little later they would have built it differently. Later still they would not have been allowed to build it here at all. It was all flat surfaces of painted concrete with big metal-frame windows and glazed metal doors. Everything was on the ground floor, though there were flat roof spaces you could use if the weather was good enough. You got to it by its own private road, and there was nothing else anywhere near it. On three sides at least the views were superb, but it must catch every wind that blew.

I suppose it gave him inspiration for his work. He wrote novels about Nelson's navy. I had not read any of them, but I remembered the name when he told me what he did. They were full of a mass of enormously authentic technical detail and highly romanticised personal relations. They were very popular, and I think he did very well out of them. He did not sail himself. His real passion was birds, and the house must have been good for that, too. I walked up there, following his instructions, having refused his offer to come and fetch me. I had not had a proper walk for some time, and it would do me all the good in the world.

The main road climbed up out of Leremouth through the woods that grew under the lee of Bonnet Point, where nine days out of ten it blew from between south and northwest. At the top the wind had wiped the great ridge clean, and there were only fields with earth-and-stone banks between them and a few lines of bowed thorn with their tops streamlined towards the southwest. It was blowing hard, and there was a tremendous yellow sunset between the flying clouds. I enjoyed the walk, but I wondered what sort of an evening lay ahead.

I left the gravel road and came through a white gate into a wind-swept garden. It was not easy to know where you were supposed to get into the house. All the windows looked like doors and the doors looked like windows. I felt sure that the house faced, if it had a face, south over the Channel, but that did not necessarily mean that the front door was on that side. I went cautiously up to what seemed a likely entrance and saw, inside the glass, Mrs. Tomlinson getting the dinner. She had her back to me. I did not see her face and she did not see me at all. I just saw that she was handsomely built, with a head of dark hair. She was very intent on what she was doing, and very serious and deliberate about it. There was none of the usual flurry of the hostess, with an apron draped over her party clothes, making sure everything is in hand before the first guests arrive. What she was doing seemed to have no reference to anybody but herself. It was a curiously intimate scene; she might have been at her dressing table. But it was only a glimpse. I backed away and continued my exploration round the house.

Then I saw Mr. Tomlinson. He was also, in his very different way, making preparations for my entertainment. He was buzzing about a big sitting room, getting drinks out. His clothes were casual but very smart. I thought it must be like living in a goldfish bowl living in that house, but perhaps they had so few visitors they did not mind. However, with that flaring yellow light outside, it was as easy to see out as it was to see in, and Mr. Tomlinson saw me almost at once. He came straight to a door in the wall of the room he was in—whether it counted as the front door I did not know—and pulled me inside. He said, "Come in, come in. Glad you found your way here. Not too much of a walk for you?"

"Not at all," I said. "I enjoyed it." I knew what I had to say next. I had to say, "This is a wonderful place you have here," but for some reason I wanted to say what I really thought about it, and I was not quite sure yet what this was. I said, "This is an astonishing position for a house."

He said, "Yes, not many like it going now. I was lucky. Come in here and see." He bustled me through into a room which filled the front of the house and which was nearly all window. Not the huge picture-windows of single glass sheets they go in for now, but nevertheless walls virtually transparent to three points of the compass. This was his working room. There was a big writing table and papers and books everywhere. There was a telescope on a tripod and a pair of enormous prismatic glasses on a bench by one of the windows. Right across the picture, and a hundred and fifty feet below us, the Channel rolled eastwards in endless crawling furrows of gold.

I said, "So this is where you watched me come round the point. I'm glad it was yesterday and not today. I shouldn't like to try it in this."

"That's it," he said. "See everything from here. No, no, no sense in going out in this. You lie snug where you are for a bit."

"I will," I said. I do not know, even now, whether there was something in the tone of his voice as he finished speaking or whether Mrs. Tomlinson's presence in some way came through to me direct. I certainly did not hear her come. All I know is that I felt an immediate need to turn and look behind me, and there she was, watching me. I put it like that because that is really how it was. She was standing quite motionless, just inside the door of the room, looking at me with concentrated attention. There was nothing surreptitious about it. Even when I turned round, she did not pretend to be doing anything else. On the contrary, when we first saw each other's faces, having both, although she did not know this, studied each other's backs, she continued for what seemed a measurable time to examine me. The odd thing was that there was no offence in it, or even any social awkwardness. You do, after all, look at people when you first meet them. But generally you talk to them at the same time, and this she did not do. I thought of her at that moment as the silent woman. Not like the Quiet Woman in the Dorset pub sign, who cannot talk because her head is off, but silent from choice. Nothing happened, in all that followed, to change this first impression of her. She was a woman whose whole instinct was to say very little, and that in a low voice. It was a sweet voice, low-pitched and very slightly husky, so that I longed to hear her use it more often.

Mr. Tomlinson said, "Oh, Helen, this is Mr. Curtis," and then she smiled, and we both said, "How do you do?" The smile and, as I have already said, the voice were both singularly sweet. She was not particularly tall, and built on generous lines, with a pale face and dark eyes under her dark hair. The whole effect was soft and deliberately muted. I found her interesting and charming. It was only gradually, during the course of the evening, that I became aware of an almost painful physical attraction. It was as though she did her best to hide it. She gave it no way at all, but it streamed out of her.

Mr. Tomlinson and I did nearly all the talking. His wife was always there, a party to the conversation. She put no constraint on it, but contributed very few words to it. I have known one or two men who had this trick, but I had never met it in a woman before. Coupled with her physical quality, I found it unbelievably disturbing.

Mr. Tomlinson's geniality did not diminish. He insisted on calling me Peter and begged me to call him Cyril. He had a well-stocked mind and practically no pretensions. He made the easiest of hosts, and she confirmed the impression I had had of her in the kitchen by putting on a meal well out of the ordinary English domestic class. It was a pleasant evening altogether. Only I did not like the house, and I did not see how anyone could. It was essentially cheerless, full of unwanted spaces and awkward angles. Even at this time of the year it was not really warm. Despite a lot of thick curtains and carpets, there was an indefinable feeling of being half out in the open. It must be pretty horrible in the winter. It was all right provided its position gave you enough pleasure to make it worth while. To Cyril Tomlinson it obviously did. I wondered about her.

But then I wondered about her altogether. You could not help wondering. There was so much you did not know about her, and yet so much you wanted, almost desperately, to know. I wondered, above all, what it would be like having her to yourself, without her husband's conversation to shield her. I wanted to make her talk, or at least do something to declare herself. It was intolerable that that obsessively desirable body should be so unforthcoming.

The wind had gone down with the sun, and I walked back down the hill in a mild air and the diffuse light of a clouded half-moon. I did not want Cyril Tomlinson to drive me back. I said I wanted the exercise, but really I wanted to be alone at once with my last impression of her. She did not come to the door, as he did. She stayed there by the log fire, saying good-bye in her quiet voice and smiling her quiet smile, and I went down the hill with practically nothing in my mind but when I should see her again and what more I could find out about her when I did.

There is a place on the hill above Leremouth where the road comes out on to a spur clear of the trees and you suddenly see the whole stretch of the estuary up-stream from the harbour. The tide was in now, and for as far as you could see, the water glimmered under the clouded moon. The low line of the dry ground showed dark beyond it, but it was impossible to see where the water ended and the dry ground began. There were no lights anywhere. It was a landscape without scale or limit, empty and completely silent. Then one of Mr. Tomlinson's birds called from out on the water, a small melancholy piping, but very clear, and the whole thing fell back into scale. The Lere estuary was not, after all, a limitless stretch of water, but it was large enough and empty of anything but birds, and in a few hours' time it would again be nothing but sand. I turned and went on down the road, making for the snug limits of the harbour and of *Madge*, floating on her moorings inside it. But I wondered why, if there was something up-stream that mattered, some place which Evan Maxwell had gone hurrying to reach while the tide was high, I could see no lights anywhere.

When I slid back the hatch and went down into it, the cabin seemed rather airless and close, and it was full of the slight, warm ghost of Celia. As I pottered about getting ready for bed, I observed with a kind of regretful detachment how slight a ghost it was. Its quick warmth and vividness were lost in the cloudy glow of Mrs. Tomlinson like colours in the moonlight. Celia was only a girl I had got fond of what seemed like a very long time ago, and might or might not have wronged. The woman up in the cold house on top of the point was the embodiment of everything a man wanted and did not understand. I put the light out and got into my bag by the faint gleam from the scuttles. For a long time I lay thinking. I felt the boat stir slightly as the ebb went out of the harbour, and I knew that outside, above the harbour, the water was falling back to uncover the great stretch of moonlit sand. There was too much to think about and there was no answer to any of it. But my walk up the hill had benefited my body, even if it had played hell with my mind, and after a time I slept.

When I woke, the cloud had come back over the sky, and it was a dark, rather cheerless day, with the promise of more rain. But I had already decided what I was going to do, and I was not going to let a little mild discomfort put me off. I put together enough food for the day, with a bottle of drinking water and a flask of hot coffee, and stowed it all in a reasonably waterproof bag under the sternsheets of the pram. I dressed lightly, with a warm guernsey on top, and took waterproofs in case I needed them. I hung a pair of field-glasses round my neck. I got into the pram and rowed out of the harbour when the morning tide was starting to make. Once outside, I turned up-stream and settled down to steady rowing, following as far as I could the course of the fresh-water stream, but knowing that in any case the tide was coming up strongly behind me.

A pram is not meant for fast travel over long distances, but it will float where nothing else will, except perhaps a rubber dinghy. I wanted to explore the estuary, going up and coming back with the tide, and I did not want to have to worry too much about the amount of water under me. If the worse came to the worst and I grounded, I should simply have to wait for the night tide to float me off. I was provisioned for it, and it would not kill me. The great thing was not to worry about time—tide, if possible, but not time.

There were birds everywhere, but no other sign of life. Every now and then I put my glasses up and looked at them. I did this a good deal at first, so that if anyone was watching me, he might be ready to believe that that was what I had come out for. Cyril Tomlinson knew that I was not in fact particularly interested in birds, but it would not be Cyril who was watching me, and no one else knew. For nearly the whole length of the estuary the steep western side was wooded, with the trees growing down almost to the water and along the high-water mark a belt of that sickly no-man's-land that you see between salt water and woodland in places of this sort. There could be anything or anyone in those woods. If I was being watched, that was where I was being watched from. On the other side there was little to be seen but sky. From down here on the water the estuary felt very vast and empty, as it had looked from above the night before. It seemed to change shape continually as I moved, particularly ahead of me, where the river wound away into the land. Every time I turned my head to look, the course ahead seemed different.

I did not really know what I was looking for, but there must be something. A bridge, perhaps, or a landing stage of some sort, even a length of road near the water. Some place where the sea made contact with the life of the land, but only at high tide and then probably very briefly. But there was nothing anywhere. Only the woods on the one hand and the marshy flats on the other, and ahead the narrowing green cleft where the Lere, no doubt a pleasant river but certainly not navigable, was absorbed in the countryside.

The tide was making strongly now. Cyril Tomlinson had been right when he said it nipped up and down a bit. At one moment I was paddling in a narrow strip of almost static water between the sand flats, and at what seemed the next there was water everywhere and the boat was drifting up-stream so fast that after a bit I simply shipped the oars and let the tide take her. I knew what time high water was supposed to be, but I did not want to trust this too far. My idea was if possible to see all there was to see while the tide was still making and then, as soon as it looked like dead water, row back hard to where I judged the central channel was and hope that the ebb would carry me down to the harbour again. Whether I should be able to get to the head of the estuary I did not know. The tides were not particularly big just now, and in a place like this an extra foot of water might mean a big difference in horizontal distance.

As I got farther up, the land on the west dropped and that on the east rose, until soon there was little to choose between them. The water lay between green banks just too high for me to see much of what lay on top of them. I had still quite a long way to go when the boat started losing way. It was getting very near the slack. Unless I was ready to risk getting left high and dry, I did not think I was going to reach the head of the estuary on this tide. Then, just as I had decided to get the oars out and start off down-stream, the high green bank on the western side fell away and there it was.

It was a house, a very old stone house, dark grey under the grey sky, sitting among trees and what looked like gardens just above the channel. It was still some way ahead, and I knew I could not get to it before I turned. I was not even sure whether this tide would come right up under it at all. But there it was, and there was nothing else. I did not know what sort of a house it was or who lived there. But I knew that it was an ordinary river-side house which, twice in every twenty-four hours, and then perhaps only if there was a big enough tide, had the sea almost under its walls. It might not mean a thing, but, as I say, there was nothing else, and it was worth looking at. But not now. Now all that mattered was to catch the ebb before it nipped down and left me. I got out the oars, turned the boat and began rowing hard down towards the centre of the channel.

CHAPTER 8

I WAS BACK ON BOARD in time to brew myself a late pot of tea. I had covered a long distance for a very small out-turn of energy, and I had at least given myself an idea that seemed worth following up. If I had been watched, I did not think I had done anything which would show where my interests lay. So far, so good. For the rest, I must move very carefully.

At all events, there was nothing more I could do today. I wondered whether I should find Cyril Tomlinson in the pub if I went along there. I wondered whether he went there every evening, and if so, what his wife did in the meantime in that chilly house up on top of the point. This set my mind moving in another direction. It was not, after all, Cyril Tomlinson that I wanted to see.

I got out paper and envelopes, and wrote a polite letter beginning *Dear Mrs. Tomlinson* and thanking her for a delightful evening. It did not matter much what I said. I might or might not gain credit for writing it, but what mattered was that it gave me a reasonable excuse for walking up and delivering it. It was long odds, anyway. Very likely Cyril Tomlinson would be at home. Even if he was not, the most I could do was to put the letter through the letter box—if, of course, they had one—and go away. If I saw Helen, it would be only by chance. Even so, it was a chance worth walking up the hill for. I finished and sealed the letter and put it in my pocket. Then I paddled ashore, left the pram in the usual place and walked up through the town towards the edge of the hanging woods.

I met no one on the road the whole way. I believe if I had heard a car coming down the hill, I should have hidden myself in the trees until it had passed, not for fear of hidden watchers, but because I was afraid Cyril might scoop me up and carry me down to spend the evening in the pub. What I should have liked best of all was to see him go down the road without seeing me. I knew now what his car looked like. But in fact nothing came at all, and I still did not know, when I got to the end of the Tomlinsons' private road, whether Cyril was at home or not, or indeed if either of them was.

It was as different as possible from the evening before. Even up here there was hardly any movement in the air, and the heavy cloud bank, which had hung over us all day but still not rained, seemed low enough to reach up and touch. The house, when I came to it, was depressing now in a different sort of way. With its sundecks and verandahs and glass walls, it looked dingy and out of place, like a man from the Punjab or the Caribbean in an English town street. I thought if there was anyone at home, they might well have lights burning, but I could not see any. I walked past what I knew was the kitchen window, but saw no one inside. I went to the door leading into the big sitting room, where I had gone in before, but there was nobody in the room. There was no letter box in the door. With the envelope in my hand and a carefully calculated look of polite bafflement on my face, I walked on round the house.

On the western side of the house, where I had not been before, there was at last a door with a letter box in it. Like all the other doors, it was mostly glass. Inside there was a small hall with doors on three sides. The door opposite would lead through into the sitting room. The flap of the letter box was stiff, as if it was not much used. I was trying to force the envelope through it when the door on the left opened and Mrs. Tomlinson came out into the hall. She came slowly, with that slight smile on her face. I stopped wrestling with the flap and stood back with the letter still in my hand. She turned a key in the lock of the door and opened it. We stood there facing each other. She was wearing some sort of housecoat belted loosely round her, and her hair was brushed out and hung almost to her waist. I wanted, more than I had ever wanted anything in my life, simply to take hold of her and pull the housecoat off her, but there was not the remotest possibility of my doing anything of the kind. She said nothing. She just stood there, smiling, and waited for me to speak.

I said, "I'm sorry. I didn't think there was anyone at home."

She held out her hand and I put the letter into it. "Only me," she said.

We still stood one on each side of the metal threshold of the metal door, looking at each other. Then she stepped back. She said, "Come in," and I went in after her. She went straight ahead and opened the door. As I had thought, we were in the big sitting room. She walked across to the sofa. There was a log fire burning in the grate. I wondered if they could ever be without fires in that house. It was almost dark, despite all the uncurtained windows, but no one suggested putting on the lights. She sat at one end of the sofa, looking up at me in that curious direct way she had, which seemed so much more concentrated because she said so little. Then she smiled again. "Sit down," she said. I sat down at the other end of the sofa, facing her. As she sat, the top of her housecoat, above the belt, opened a little, so that I could see the beginning of the cleft between her breasts. I have never seen such a skin on any woman. It was perfectly white, and yet I thought I could almost feel the warmth of it. There was no deliberate provocation in this at all. She must have known how I felt, because no woman could miss that strength of feeling in a man. But she seemed to take it for granted, as if there was in any case nothing to be done about it.

She said suddenly, "Where have you come from?"

"Now?" I said. "From the harbour."

She shook her head. "I mean in your boat," she said.

"Oh—up the coast, from Cornwall." I knew that she could not have the wrong reasons for asking. She lived here. I had met her only because I had met her husband, and I had met him by chance, because I had decided to go into one pub rather than another. All the same, I did not want to tell her what I had been doing with my life these last few years. Or not yet. Perhaps later, when I knew her better, if I ever did. But not yet.

She said, "You're on holiday?"

"More or less."

She looked at me for a moment or two. Then she nodded. I knew it was time I got up and went, but I could not bring myself to leave her. People talk of attraction far too easily. This was as palpable as gravity. She held up my letter, which she had had in her hand ever since we came in. "Do you want me to read this?" she said.

"Not really." She smiled then, and I said what I had had no intention of saying. "It was only an excuse," I said. "It's quite correct and unexceptionable. But it's only an excuse for coming. I wanted to see you."

She knew that, of course. She must have known it. She opened the envelope and took out the letter. She screwed up the envelope, spread the letter out and put it on the arm of the sofa beside her. She did not read it. She said, "I thought perhaps you'd come back with Cyril."

"But you knew I'd come?"

"I thought so, yes."

"Do you mind?"

"I don't know." She got up and I got up too, but I still did not move away from her. "I'll have to think about it," she said.

I was between her and the door. She could not move towards the door without coming closer to me, and she knew she must not do that. She said, "Please go." It was hardly above a whisper, but it was full of an almost desperate urgency. I forced myself, as if by a muscular effort, to turn away from her. I turned away and walked to the door. I opened it and went out into the hall. She came after me and stood in the sitting-room doorway. She said, "We don't use this much, I'm afraid."

"Doesn't anyone ever come here?" I said.

She shook her head. "There's no one to come."

I pulled open the outer door. I was unnecessarily violent with it. I was suddenly very angry, angry with Cyril Tomlinson and the whole impossible situation. I went outside and turned round. She was still standing in the sitting-room doorway. "There is now," I said.

She nodded. She did not seem to be accepting anything, merely recognising a fact. "All right," she said.

I shut the door and went off towards the road along the west side of the house. I looked into the window on my right, because that was the room she had come out of. It was a small bedroom with a single bed and a dressing table covered with the usual feminine gear. I said to myself, "She had been getting ready. She expected me to come later, and she had been getting ready." I did not know whether it was true or not, but once I had had the idea, I could not bear to disbelieve it. I walked to the gate. When I got on to the private road, I almost ran. The one thing I could not face was the possibility of meeting Cyril Tomlinson and having to go back to the house with him. As I was going down through the woods, I twice heard cars coming up the hill, and both times I turned off into the trees and let them go by. I did not know if either of them was his.

I thought of going and buying myself a drink, and perhaps a meal, but I hesitated. I wanted to be either completely alone or very much in company, but I could not decide which. I did not in any case want to go to the same pub—it was the Anchor, in fact—in case Cyril Tomlinson was still there. I did not think he could be. I thought he would have gone back up the hill by now. So as not, as he would say, to catch it. I tried to imagine, now, what his catching it would consist of. What did Helen Tomlinson do when this educated, kindly, likable man came home a little late and a little drunk from his harmless evening talking to Fred and the locals in the Anchor? What, in God's name, went on between them, him with his concrete dream-house and his cheerfulness and his esoteric areas of knowledge, and her with her dignity and her silence and the desperate need to be loved which—I could not be wrong about this—radiated almost visibly from her dark eyes and white body? I walked, without consciously making any decision, to the pier steps and down to the waiting pram.

There was an envelope addressed to me pinned with a drawing pin to the centre thwart. Of all utterly unreasonable things, I at once thought of Celia. I suppose it was because of that early morning, over a week ago, when I had hoped, God knows why, to find a message from her in the pram when I had swum across to it in Carristowe harbour. This was from Cyril Tomlinson, of course. I had not seen his writing, but it was exactly what it would be, small and well formed and fluent, the hand of a man who wrote a lot, but (perhaps only at this hour of the evening) a little irregular and oddly spaced. The envelope was borrowed from the Anchor and had the brewer's name on it. I unpinned it from the thwart and pushed the drawing pin carefully into the gunwale. I cannot bear to throw away a thing like that. *Dear Peter,* he had written, *I've been hoping to see you, but you didn't show up. They tell me you've been up river. Hope you didn't get stuck. I was going to ask you to come up and have a meal. Helen will be sorry. Come up tomorrow, if I don't see you in the meantime. Yours, Cyril.*

I put the paper back in the envelope and the envelope in my pocket. Then I got out the oars and paddled over to *Madge*. All this letter-writing, I thought. But my heart was beating a shade quicker, and I felt slightly hollow in my stomach. There were two things here that upset me. I thought they were two separate and unconnected upsets, but I could not be quite certain. They, whoever they were, knew I had been up-river. And Cyril knew that Helen would be sorry I had not come.

I got aboard and lit the stove and set about getting myself a meal. All the time I turned the two things over in my head. The first, the more I came to think of it, was nothing to get upset about. In a place the size of Leremouth of course my trip up-river would not have gone unnoticed. And there had been no systematic watching. Whoever they were, they did not even know when I had come back. This had upset me only because I was expecting to be watched and because I was uneasily involved in the business which led me to expect it.

The other thing was different. Helen Tomlinson had said she thought I might come back with Cyril. I had assumed, because this was what I wanted to think, that this had been something in her own mind, which she had kept to herself until she had told me about it. It was disconcerting to think that she might have discussed it with her husband. I had the picture of his suggesting an extra to dinner and her agreeing unwillingly to water the soup. But I did not, even then, believe this. My mind threw it up, in the way one's mind does throw up the thing one least wants to believe or contemplate. But I rejected it not only because I so much disliked it, but because it was against the evidence. On the other hand, if he had not discussed it with her, why did Cyril say that she would be sorry if I did not come? It could be the merest of polite formulas, but that was not like him. If he said Helen would be sorry, he really thought she would be. Now that I had gone up and spoken to her, I myself thought she would have been disappointed if I had not come at all. But I did not like his knowing this. More unreasonably, but quite unmistakably, I did not like the fact that he did not seem to mind. I wondered, suddenly and for the first time, how long they had been married, but there did not seem to be any way of finding out.

Meanwhile, I had been invited to dine with the Tomlinsons again tomorrow evening, and of course I should go. I should go because I wanted to see Helen whenever I could and whatever the circumstances. I should go with this element of unease in my mind and with questions I wanted answered. But I could not keep away.

It was hot in the cabin with the stove going. I left it on, but when I had finished with the supper things, I put on a guernsey and went up into the cockpit to smoke a pipe. There was still no wind, but the cloud had gone and the sky was full of stars. The lights of the town stood in rows above the harbour, but above them the dark bank of trees showed no lights at all. Somewhere over the crest of the hill there would be lights of a sort showing from the house on top of the point, but you could not see them from here. I believe if I had had a car, I should have driven up the hill, not to talk to either Cyril or Helen, but to see them if I could, simply to watch what they did and how they behaved when I was not there with them. I was obsessed with the mystery of their relation, and there they were in a glass box in the middle of a dark wilderness. But I knew it was lunacy, and the mere physical barrier was a sufficient argument for sanity.

I turned my mind to the business which had brought me to Leremouth. It did not seem to be of much importance compared with what had happened to me since I got there. All the same, I did not think it could be left. I thought in the morning I would go and look at the house at the head of the estuary. But this time I would not go by water. I knocked out my pipe on the topsides of the boat and went down to bed.

CHAPTER 9

I DO NOT THINK, this time, that anyone knew where I was. I had gone into the town early and done some shopping. I had taken the stuff back to the boat and then, rather as if I had forgotten something, brought the pram back to the steps and gone into the town again. But this time I had wandered off into the northeastern corner, where the houses petered out against the high bank of the river. There was a path of sorts running across the grass slope towards where the trees began. I sauntered along it with my hands in my pockets and what I hoped was the manner of a man who was walking but not going anywhere. The tide was making fast, but when I reached the trees there was still sand at the bottom of the bank. I turned off the path and went down to look at it.

Here, near the side, it was firm enough, of course. It would be only a topcoat of sand with soil not far beneath. It was full of branches and bits of cut timber, scoured smooth and white as bones, and there were soaked leaves and rusting tins and up-ended bottles, the mixed debris of the woods up-stream and the town below. There were probably the stumps of trees under the sand, with their roots still in the soil. In places like this I have seen a freak tide leave a stretch of foreshore looking like a forest clearing. Farther out in the middle, where it had been nothing but sand for a long time and the subsoil was irretrievably sunk, there might well be places where it was better not to walk. As Cyril Tomlinson had said, you would want to know it. But for the moment I was not interested in the middle of the river. I had seen that already.

I pottered up along the sand until the trees closed in over me. Then I walked on another twenty yards or so, climbed up the slope of slippery soil and sat down with my back against the first tree with reasonably dry ground under it. Then I waited.

The fine weather was coming back. The sky was slightly hazed, but there was a gentle breeze blowing up-river, and I reckoned that up here this meant a true southerly. Presently the sky would clear and the sun would be hot enough to warm some of the sand before the tide closed over it. It was of course perfect sailing weather, and before long it might occur to someone to wonder why I did not continue my voyage eastwards up the coast. The answer to that, I thought, must be in the Tomlinsons and their hospitality. Cyril obviously lacked company of his own kind, and I did not imagine I was the first visitor he had seized on and urged to drop his hook for a little and come up to the house for meals. This would be known locally, if anyone was sufficiently interested to enquire. I wondered, then, about Helen, and a small pang of pure jealousy jabbed me suddenly in that indeterminate region under the heart where these things make themselves felt. I did not like to think that there had been that same intensity of feeling between Helen and some earlier visitor that I thought there was between her and me. There was no sense in this, but it is common enough. God knows I was not the first man to take the husband in his stride and concentrate his resentment on an imagined outside competitor. But he was a shadowy figure at best and I did not waste much time on him. Meanwhile, there must be no more lurking in the trees when I was on my way up the hill. The more people who knew about it, the better. Cyril, of course, would know too. But Cyril did not seem to mind. Or not so far. But this was nonsense. So far there was nothing for him to mind.

All this time nothing stirred. The trees whispered faintly in the breeze, and the sun shone brighter and brighter on the flat water that came swirling in over the sands. But there was no human figure anywhere. Whether or not anyone had seen me leave the town, no one, now, could know exactly where I was. I got up and started to make my way up between the trees, heading for the main road.

The slope was surprisingly steep, and at times I had almost to get hold of the tree trunks and pull myself up between them. I stopped twice to get my breath back, and the second time, just when I was going to start climbing again, I heard the sound of a car above me. The sound came and went, muffled by the trees, but I did not think the car, at its nearest point, had been very far away. Presently I saw sunlight through the trees, and then, almost at once, another car passed. It was so close that I almost ducked, but I saw nothing. There was only one explanation. The road must be cut well into the side of the hill, with perhaps a near-vertical face above it and a sharp fall below. I should have to get almost to the edge of the shelf before my head was even on a level with the tarmac.

This suited me very well. I had some way to go, and my only hope of doing it in a reasonable time was to walk on the road. But I did not want to be seen, if possible not at all. We have already reached a point where a man walking along an ordinary road is an object of curiosity. If his clothes and trappings make this sufficiently obvious, he may be assumed to be walking for pleasure, or at least of set purpose. If not, it is taken for granted that he wants to stop walking and get himself into a car as soon as possible. If he shows no signs of this, there is something odd about him, and the drivers who pass him will notice and remember him. I did not want a lift, and I did not want to be noticed and remembered. My only hope was to make what speed I could along the edge of the tarmac and plunge down the slope when I heard a car coming. There were not many cars on the road, and in that tunnel of trees you could hear them coming a good way off. It was a bit taxing but perfectly feasible. In the first mile or so only half a dozen cars came along, and none of them got a sight of me.

The road ran pretty well parallel with the bank of the river, and I was making good speed in the direction I wanted to go. I had been walking, with interruptions, for about three quarters of an hour when the trees began to thin out below me, so that I could see the sand and an occasional gleam of water through them. Very soon after this the road began to go down-hill and I could see open country ahead. It was time to get down to the bank of the river again. I left the road for the last time and went straight down through the trees. The slope was easier here and the trees thinner. When I got to the bottom, I found fields, fenced with the usual earth banks, going right to the edge of the river. Beyond them, perhaps a quarter of a mile up-stream, I knew that there was this dip in the ground, perhaps where a side stream ran down to the river. The house was at the bottom of the dip, just over the water so long as the water was there. There would be a lane or drive connecting it with the road, but I did not think it need be a very long one.

I came to the edge of the trees and stopped. The tide was making with its usual speed. It already covered all the middle of the estuary and, at least where I was, would soon be up to the bank. At about this point, as I already knew, it came up against a shelving bottom and slowed down a lot. I still did not know whether, as the tides were now, it would reach the house or not. There was no one about in the fields ahead of me. Whether I could be seen from the road I doubted, but in any case it was a risk I had to take. I struck straight out over the fields.

I saw the tops of the trees first and then, a moment later, the roof of the house itself. There was a bank in front of me, but no gate that I could see in this side of the field. I scrambled up the bank and then, half kneeling, put my head over the top. The house was smaller than I had thought when I had seen it from out on the river, not much more than a fair-sized farmhouse originally. Now there were a few stone out-buildings round it, but there was no sign of its being used as a farm. It stood among its own bunch of trees close to the side of the river. There was, as I had thought, a bit of garden round it on the other three sides. There was a low stone wall with a gate in it between the garden and the fields inland. The gate would be where the track came in across the fields from the main road, but I could not see it.

I could see no sign of life at all. It was all completely quiet. It did not look derelict, but I found it difficult to believe that very much went on there. I climbed over the bank and went across another field, until there was only one field left between me and the garden wall. Then I turned right-handed and went down to the edge of the river. The tide was already closer to the bank than I had expected. I thought that all except the smallest neap tides would come up under the house, and the house was ready for it. The bank was faced solidly with stone, and I should be surprised if there were not steps going down to the sand and perhaps mooring rings let into the stone. There was nothing in the way of a boat there now. I went right down the bank and walked cautiously along the sand, with the tide lapping only a few yards away on my right hand.

As I had thought, the wall came right down to the sand. It was old stonework, as old as the house, and ten or twelve feet high, with a recessed flight of steps half-way along it. Given a decent high tide, you could bring a boat alongside and take on or land anything or anybody. But you would not, whatever the state of the tides was, have very long to do it. Unless you wanted to be left high and dry under the wall, you would have to be off and away down-river while there was still water under you. I did not know whether it was an arrival or a departure he had been interested in, but I thought that this was where Evan Maxwell had intended to be on that late June evening four years ago. It might still be all moonshine, but nothing else seemed to make sense. I stopped, listened, heard nothing but the birds singing in the garden trees and went quietly up the steps.

The front of the house stared straight at me across a few garden beds with a flagged path running through them. The windows were there, glazed, closed, with even a hint of curtain drawn back at the sides, but I did not, even at a first glance, believe there was anybody inside them. I suppose in fact it was the garden rather than the house itself that gave me this immediate but overwhelming impression of a place not abandoned but not used. It takes time for a properly built house to show signs of neglect, but a garden can get out of hand in a matter of months. This was not out of hand. The beds were forked over and clean, the path clear of weeds. But there was nothing in the beds but a few rose-bushes, which needed pruning, but were in thick flower. That was what the whole place smelt of—the salty rottenness of the tidal banks and the clusters of unkempt roses. Nobody lived there, but somebody looked after it.

I did not know if there was anything more to be learnt, but I went on up the path, treading quietly because the whole place was so quiet. It was dark inside the windows, but the rooms were not empty. There was furniture, some of it dust-sheeted, and carpets rolled back. I turned right-handed along the front of the house. There was a stone arch at that side, with a small gate under it, which would take me round to the back. The drop-latch of the gate was rusty and did not lift when I tried it. I got my whole hand under it and pressed. It flew up with a loud click, and a dog began barking at the back of the house.

It was a big dog. A bark like that came out of a deep chest. The one thing I could not do was go back. If there was anyone with the dog, they would almost certainly see me anyhow, and the man who retreats when a dog barks is either unduly scared of dogs or up to no honest purpose. I was not prepared to admit that I was either. I went through the gate and then, perhaps as a gesture to myself, shut it behind me. The latch clicked again, and the dog, who had stopped to listen, started barking again. I followed the path along the gable wall. As I moved I realised that the barking was getting louder, and a moment later the dog came round the corner of the house.

My heart missed a beat and I said, "Sam!" Of course it was not Sam. Sam had been dead these four years, but it was a big black Labrador terribly like him. I dropped on my knees and held out my arms to him. No decent Labrador will go for a kneeling man unless he has been taught to. The dog pulled up a yard in front of me. He gave one more bark, but only because it had already been in the pipeline. It was the noise he had been barking at, not me. With me here, in front of him, he had to make up his mind. It did not take him long. The wave of appalling affection that flowed out of me hit him almost visibly, and the great tail began to flag from side to side. In another second he was in my arms. Like most of his kind, he was a glutton for affection. It was several seconds before I was aware that there was a man standing at the corner of the house. He had a shotgun in his hands, but already the gun was pointing at the ground. I lifted my head and looked at him, with the silly tears of a grown man running down my face.

He looked at me. He was in a fair state of confusion, but already the situation was well out of his control. It was his dog. Whoever said, "Love me, love my dog," had got his priorities badly mixed. It is that sort of sentimentality that gives dog-lovers a bad name. What is true is that if your dog takes to someone, you have to have very solid reasons for disliking him. Despite his shotgun, the man had nothing against me, except that I was where I was. All he could see was a large man crying over his dog and the dog licking the large man where he could get at him. No wonder he was confused. I was beginning to feel pretty foolish myself.

I disentangled myself from the dog and got to my feet. I said, "I'm sorry." I was of course apologising for crying, not for being where I was. That could come later. What I had to deal with first was this appalling breach in the established canons of behaviour. "I had one very like him," I said. "I lost him."

The man nodded, fighting with his sympathy as you fight with rising anger or sudden fear. He said, "Ah." He broke the gun and tucked it under his arm. He said, "C'mere, Jack." The dog was still visibly caught between two poles of affection. He rolled back to his master, flagging his tail in a circle and grinning in both our faces. "I heard him barking," the man said. "I wondered what it was."

We were back to the business of the day. For the second time I apologised. "I'm sorry," I said. "I was walking along the river and saw the steps and came up. There didn't seem to be anybody about."

"You came up the steps?" he said.

"That's right. I thought—"

"The tide'll be on 'em soon."

"Yes. Yes, it's making pretty fast. I was wondering—could I get back to the road this way?"

He considered this, not, of course, as a matter of physical possibility, but as a question of right. "Well," he said, "you could. There's a track up to the road." He jerked his head over his shoulder. "It's a private right of way. The field's not ours. But now you're here—"

He turned, and we started to walk round the back of the house, with Jack almost under our feet. I looked among the buildings for a cottage the man might be living in, but I could not see anything. "It's a lovely place," I said. "Quiet. You live here?"

He looked at me pretty sharply, but I was busy admiring the house. "Well," he said. "Not regular. I keep an eye on it, like."

"Aha. Holiday house, is it?" I knew this was not true, but it would stand correction.

He could not let it pass. "Oh no," he said. "Always been lived in. But the owner died a few years back, and it seems they haven't made up their minds what they want done with it."

I made sympathetic noises. "Pity," I said. "Lovely place like that." I smiled at him. "I envy you your job," I said.

"Well," he said, "I don't know. I used to work regular for Mr. Casson, of course. Now I don't know."

We came to the gate in the ring wall I had seen from across the fields. The track ran straight ahead, slightly up-hill, to where the road would be. I said, "I'll be getting on, then. Thank you for letting me come through. I'm sorry I disturbed you." I put my hand down for Jack, who put his great head up against my knees and grinned at me while I rubbed his ears. The coat was like silk. " 'Bye, Jack," I said. I was almost speechless again. I waved a hand to the man and went off across the fields.

The man's cottage was by the gate where the track joined the road. I turned left and walked quickly up the hill to where the trees began. Nothing passed me in either direction. When I came to the trees, I went as I had come, avoiding the traffic. Unless I was completely wrong, the people who might be watching me could not know about the house. The man might report my visit to the people who owned it, but they could not be the same people. There had to be a connection somewhere, but only I knew this. Evan Maxwell had known it, and now I knew it, but as far as I could make out, no one else did.

A quarter of a mile or so outside Leremouth I turned down into the woods and went straight down to the bank of the river. It was full flood now. The great sheet of water stretched unbroken from the flats on the far side almost to the roots of the trees. I began to walk back along the high-water mark, just clear of where the water was now, picking my way through the rotten stuff and the muddy pebbles and stepping over the derelict branches. When there was only a hundred yards to go, I turned and clambered up the slippery bank into the bottom of the wood.

There was an enormous pair of field-glasses staring almost into my face. They were lowered and Cyril Tomlinson looked at me from behind them. His face was more nearly hostile than I had imagined it could be. He said, "What the hell are you up to? There's a pair of Caspian terns out on the water there. Or that's what it looks like. You'll have them up in a minute. Get down, for God's sake."

I nodded but did not say anything. I went round behind him and sat down with my back against a tree. He had his glasses up again. Silence fell. I made myself comfortable and tried to think.

CHAPTER 10

Cyril Tomlinson said, "I'm sorry if I was a bit fierce with you this morning. It was the Caspians. I'd only just spotted them, and they're pretty rare visitors."

"Not a bit," I said. "I'm sorry I nearly frightened them away. I hadn't even seen them, of course. And I shouldn't have known what they were if I had."

Helen looked quickly at her husband and then at me. "Where was this?" she said.

The thing that struck me was that she really wanted to know. If she had not, she would not have asked. It also seemed a little odd that Cyril should not have mentioned it to her earlier. Perhaps he did not mention things like that to her. It was one of the many things I did not know about them. Even now it was me she had asked, not Cyril. "Down on the river," I said. "Only a little up-stream from the harbour." I looked at her and she looked back at me. Her face seemed the only thing I could see in focus. Everything else, the table, the whole lamp-lit room, seemed only the periphery of that pale face and those great dark eyes. I went on talking, but I heard my voice as if it belonged to someone else. "I'd been walking on the edge of the water, and when I came up the bank, there was this great pair of glasses with Cyril behind them. It was like being held up at gunpoint. My instinct was to duck. Which was what he wanted anyway."

And I love you, I love you, I said to her eyes, you are the most wonderful woman I have ever seen. Let me love you a little. "So I sat down quietly behind him till he'd seen all he wanted to see," I said. I smiled at her, but she did not smile back, or only very slightly.

"He was a model of forbearance," said Cyril.

Her eyes turned to him, and the room came back into focus again. She had one white arm resting on the dark wood of the table.

"All the same," he said, "I'm glad you were close under the bank. Not that you could have been anywhere else at that state of the tide. But don't go walking out into the middle at low tide, not by yourself. It's not safe unless you know it."

"Real quicksands?"

"Well—I don't think anyone's ever gone right down in them. But you could get pretty well stuck in places. And with the tide coming in the way it does, it wouldn't be so funny. We've had plenty of people drowned. Visitors, mostly. Well—the tide doesn't move all that fast and the distances aren't all that big. It was just that they tried to get away and couldn't. I think what happens is that the water comes up under the sand as well as over it. One moment you're on firm going, and the next it just gives under you. The thing to do, of course, would be to lie flat and wait for the tide to lift you, and then swim for it. But it would need a bit of nerve, and most people wouldn't think of it. Anyway, if you were well out, it would be quite a swim."

Helen said, "I'd rather you didn't go up the river at all." She said it to me, but her eyes flickered sideways to Cyril, and for a moment they looked at each other.

"Quite right," he said. "It isn't awfully safe, and that's a fact."

I laughed at him. I did not look at her at all. "Bah," I said, "it's the birds you're worrying about. You don't want anyone trepassing on your preserves." Then, when I had said it, I wondered how closely he guarded his other preserves, and I looked at Helen and found her looking at me. I thought she knew perfectly well what was in my mind, but there was nothing conspiratorial in her look at all. She had said, "I'll have to think about it," and she was still thinking. I could only wait.

Cyril said, "There's plenty of room for the birds. I only don't want you to drown yourself. What about coffee? Shall I make it?"

Helen said, "Yes, please," and he bustled off. I thought he was the sort of man who would do things like that very well. He was probably a good cook, too. With Helen's cooking what it was, it was a talent he would not have to exercise very often, but at least it meant that he would know how good hers was. In all those ways they suited each other very well. It was the other ways I wondered about.

She settled herself at her usual end of the sofa by the side of the fire. I sat on a chair opposite her, for choice, because from there I could look at her without being too obvious about it when Cyril came back with the coffee. She said, "You're rather a mysterious person."

"I was afraid I was being rather obvious."

She smiled and shook her head. It was as if we were in some way at cross-purposes, but she did not say how.

"The mystery is in you," I said. "You can't spend anything like as much time wondering about me as I spend wondering about you." She sat there, rather straight, with her hands folded in her lap and those wonderful arms modelled against the dark stuff of her dress. She was perfectly still. The stillness went with the silence. She moved, as she spoke, beautifully, but deliberately and of set purpose, when the need was there. "Are you happy?" I said.

She had been looking into the fire. She moved hardly more than her eyes and looked at me for a moment. Then she looked away again. After a bit she said, "I'm not unhappy."

"You could be happy." I did not say, I do not think I even meant, the fatuous male "I could make you happy." I was conscious, all the time I was with her, of some tremendous potential which I knew was never realised, and I could not bear that it should be left unrealised. In a way I was jealous, not of any person I knew of, but of the mere possibility that the rest of the world might apprehend in her what I had apprehended. It seemed to me impossible that it could be missed. At least I had to make her understand that I had not missed it. I said again, "You could be happy," and then Cyril came in with the coffee tray.

He brought brandy with it, a full bottle and glasses for all three of us. He poured out a very reasonable dram and handed it to Helen. He did not ask her if she wanted it, and she took it without comment. Then he poured out two outrageous measures for himself and me. It was all quiet and deliberate and done with a curious air of intentness. After what we had already had, this was going to make us measurably drunk, him certainly, myself almost certainly. I did not know about Helen. I could not imagine her drunk at all. But whatever he thought would happen, the action was, as I say, deliberate.

I did not mind. I had only to walk to the harbour steps, and could trust myself, drunk or sober, to get on board without drowning myself. But that was all away in an incalculably remote future. Here and now two at least of us were going to get drunk, and something might emerge, some barrier might go down, I might find my way to some of the things I wanted to know. I took my glass, like Helen, without comment, sniffed it and put it aside while I drank my coffee. As I had thought, the coffee was perfect. I know much less about brandy, but when I at last sipped it, I found it smoother and headier than anything I could ever remember drinking. Just before I sipped, I looked at Helen over the top of my glass. She had her glass to her lips, but she, too, had not yet drunk. I do not think either of us moved our glasses, but we looked at each other for what seemed a very long time. Then she smiled very slightly and tilted her glass to drink. I drank too, and all the time I held her eyes, and her eyes smiled at me while her mouth sipped.

I do not know how much, by the end of it, we had really drunk. I know Cyril poured out at least twice more, and each time Helen drank with us, less than we drank, but still a fair amount. All the time Cyril talked, and I talked with him, and Helen said hardly a word, and all the time with three parts of my mind I concentrated on her as I have never concentrated on any creature or thing. There was moonlight outside now, and a wind blowing hard against the house. I did not know when it had started or how long it had been blowing, but it seemed part of the speed and confusion of my mind. High above this confusion, at some remote and detached level, I spoke to Cyril with the tremendous verbal precision of the introvert drunk, and made small deliberate movements with my hands and my glass, like a tightrope walker demonstrating his control by opening and shutting an umbrella or doing something equally irrelevant to the business of balancing himself on his high wire.

Then there was a tremendous crash in the next room, and Cyril got up and said, "My God, that's a window slammed."

I got up too and said, "Yes, I think it must be," only by that time Cyril was almost to the door, weaving between the furniture with dazzling virtuosity and his glass still in his hand.

He opened the door and went through it, and I turned and found Helen standing just behind me. We clung to each other and kissed, a long kiss of total surrender to circumstance. Then I let go of her and turned and went after Cyril.

The window was not broken, but there was a fair amount of confusion. It was a casement window that had got loose from its catch and slammed open. There were papers flying everywhere in the moonlit room, and a curtain had wrapped itself round the telescope on its tripod and was threatening to have the whole thing down. I shut the door, which Cyril had left open, and grappled with the telescope while he leant out into the wild night and forced the window back against the rush of air. Presently he banged it shut and fastened it, and there was a sudden silence. He went across the room with a sort of despairing deliberation and switched on a light. Then he looked round and said, "My God, what a mess. Never mind. It will keep." There was no exasperation in him, even now, only a sort of gentle acceptance of disaster. He picked up his glass from the top of a bookcase near the door. It still had some brandy in it. He had not spilled a drop. We went back into the sitting room. Helen was no longer there. Her glass was on the tray, empty. Mine was on the table. It had been empty when I put it down.

I said, "I must be going."

"Yes," he said. "All right. But it will be all right in the harbour. You don't have to worry about the boat."

I said, "No. No, I'm not worrying about the boat. But I must be going."

"I'll see you out," he said.

We got ourselves out into the garden. It was blowing almost due west. The sky was full of wisps of cloud belting across the moon, and the sea was a vast continuous shimmer. We got to the gate and he opened it and let me out. Then he shut it from the inside and stayed there, holding on to it. He was perfectly all right on his feet, even in that wind, but he seemed to want something to hold on to. He said, "I must go back. Helen doesn't like a wind."

"No?" I said. "You must get a lot of wind here."

He nodded. "Yes. Yes, that's it. I don't think she really likes it here."

I locked this carefully into my mind, but I wanted to comfort him. I said, "You must both be used to it by now."

"Not really. She hasn't been here long. Only two years. I don't think she's got used to it."

I could not find anything to say to this. We stood there in the raging moonlight, I on the grit road and he inside the gate. It was as if he was the prisoner and I the free one, and yet all I wanted was inside that gaunt white house and I was shut outside. I said, "Say good night to Helen for me," and he said,

"Yes, yes, I will," and I turned and walked off along the road. I walked perhaps fifty yards, and then I stopped and turned back. There was no sense in it, but I could not go, not just yet. Only two years, he had said. And he had said she, not we. He must have been here much longer. They had been married only two years, and she had to kiss like that.

When I came back to the gate, I leant on it, as he had, only on the outside, staring at the long shape of the house dappled with the racing cloud shadows. From here I could see no lights in it at all. I remembered once, when I was very young, standing outside a house in the moonlight like that, unable to leave it because of someone inside. I remembered the house but not the person. When all the windows are dark, a house looks more close and secretive in the moonlight than at any other time. I do not know how long I stayed there, leaning on the gate. I think it was quite a long time, because suddenly I realised that I was very cold. I opened the gate and went into the garden. I did not think there would be anybody to see me now. I began to walk round the edge of the garden, moving round the house, but keeping well away from it.

All the lights were out. The house was dead and everyone in it asleep, if they could sleep with the wind roaring on the roof and all this brilliance outside. I walked very slowly all round the house, as if I was trying to cast a spell on it, and came back to the gate. I was tired now, and I still had to walk back to the harbour. I told myself I would walk round it once more, quite quickly, and then leave it and go away. When I came to the front of the house, Helen was standing against the wall, sheltered from the wind, in the full light of the moon. She came across and took me by the hand, and we went down a path leading out from the garden towards the end of the point. The path dropped until we were out of sight of the house, and then we stopped and made love on the grass in the tempestuous moonlight, with the wind blowing our clothes all over the place.

I do not think we spoke the whole time. She abandoned herself totally, not to me, but to whatever was driving her, in a sort of agony of surrender that seemed more than anything like grief. I do not suppose she would have done it with anyone, but I did not at any moment believe it had very much to do with me. I might have been a creature of her own imagination or a god come up out of that raging sea to serve her. Only when it was over and we were walking back up the path, she suddenly turned and picked up my hand and kissed it lightly, as if she had suddenly realised I was there and was grateful. When we came to the house, she touched my hand once more and went inside. I walked round to the gate and this time I shut it behind me and walked straight off along the road without looking back.

The town and harbour lay locked in the moonlight. The wind here was all erratic eddies of air chasing each other in the lee of the cliffs and the huge bank of trees. The water was ruffled and the boats moved restlessly on their moorings, but there was no violence in it. I must still have had a lot of Cyril Tomlinson's brandy in me, but I did not feel in the least drunk, only rather light-headed. Nothing seemed very real. To all the senses the world was full of magic, but underneath it I was aware of a tremendous disquiet. There was too much happening, and to me, that I did not understand. I had come to Leremouth for a secret purpose of my own, but I was beginning to feel that the secrets were not all mine and that I was no longer in control of the situation.

I rowed out to where *Madge*, as white as a ghost ship in the moonlight, rocked gently on the dark water. Here at least I was safe and on my own again. I believe if conditions had been different, I might have got sail up and gone. But there was nowhere to go except the tormented sea outside and the great reach of shallow treacherous water up-stream, and there was nothing for it but to stay where I was. I made the pram fast and went below. I switched on the lights and pulled the hatch to. I had had enough of the moonlight.

The brandy had given me a thirst, and I went to the galley to get myself a drink. The first glass I put my hand on had a faint mark of pinkish lipstick on its rim. I looked at it for a moment and then put it back. That was long ago and in a far country. I found another glass and filled and drained it three times to run the brandy out of my system. Then I got to bed.

CHAPTER 11

It was a dark morning and blowing harder than ever. I woke late and lay for some time on my berth, staring up at the varnished woodwork over me and listening to the sounds *Madge* made as she rocked on her moorings. I had no hangover to speak of. Cyril's brandy must have been very good. But I was not happy.

I was not only physically obsessed with Helen. I was in love with her, and what had happened up there on the moonlit cliff was little comfort to a man in love. The desperate physical tension was broken, but I was no nearer knowing her. It was not me she had surrendered to. I supposed, now that the barrier was down, I might find my way gradually into her mind, but I was not at all sure of this. That one kiss on the back of my hand as we were on our way up to the house meant more to me than everything that happened first, and a quick, almost absent-minded kiss on the back of the hand is not much to be going on with. I had to see her again, in case there was anything more to it than that. I got up and set about the business of the day. I made myself coffee, which was all I wanted. I was just putting the things away when I heard the whistle.

I slid back the hatch and climbed up into the cockpit. Cyril was standing at the top of the steps. He waved when he saw me and I waved back. I felt very hollow and uncertain what was going to happen, but there was only one thing I could do. I pulled the pram in and paddled across to him. As I came in to the steps, he came down them. He said, "Are you all right? I was worried about you."

I sat there, holding on to the wet stonework with one hand while the pram went up and down a little on the popple in the harbour, and looked up at him. Once again, and even now, the concern was genuine. I could not be wrong about this. "I'm all right," I said.

"Well, thank God for that. Only—we drank a bit, and with the wind coming up like that—"

"I'd sobered up by the time I got down here."

"I suppose so." He hesitated, looking down at me uncertainly. "I wondered—you coming into town? I could do with a hair of the dog."

"I tell you what," I said. "You come aboard and I'll give you coffee at least, and anything else you want, if it comes to that."

He was very pleased at that. His whole face radiated surprise and pleasure, like a child's. "That's very nice of you," he said, "if I won't be a nuisance."

"No nuisance at all. I owe you hospitality, in all conscience." I took the oars and turned the stern of the pram in to the steps. He stepped in and sat down neatly enough for a man who did no sailing. He knew about boats, of course. But mainly it was because there was so little self-consciousness in him. He had none of the ordinary adult's fear of doing the wrong thing in an unfamiliar setting. He took the obvious line, as a child does, instinctively and without fuss. When we got to *Madge*, he scrambled aboard and took the end of the painter, while I stowed the oars and rowlocks. He did not attempt to make the pram fast, but he held it until I was out of it and then handed the painter to me. After that he clambered about the boat asking questions. They were intelligent questions, and he understood the answers. I felt like a character in a Kipling story explaining modern sailing practice to a returned eighteenth-century expert.

Finally I got him settled below and asked him what he wanted.

He looked at me doubtfully and said, "I suppose you haven't got any beer on board? That's really what I need."

"Of course," I said. I produced a bottle for his inspection. "That any good to you?"

"That would be marvellous. I'm afraid—" he looked at me doubtfully again—"I'm afraid I was a bit drunk last night. I remember meaning to be, and I think I must have been."

"You were no drunker than I was. We both drank a lot of your lovely brandy. But you were perfectly under control. I found it very impressive."

He nodded. We waved our glasses at each other and drank. He took most of his down in one long pull, drinking with his eyes almost shut. Then he shivered and came to the surface. "Thank God for that," he said. He put his glass down carefully where the slight rocking of the boat would not upset it. While he was still busy with it, he said, "What happened?"

I looked at him carefully, and after a moment he stopped fiddling with his glass and looked across at me. "What happened when?" I said.

"When you went," he said. For what seemed a very long time no one said anything. Then he said, "I went with you to the gate. I think we stayed talking. What did I say?"

I lifted my glass and drank. My hand was not perfectly steady. I tried desperately not to look relieved. I was still, in fact, worried, but there was a way clear ahead and I took it. "You didn't say much," I said. "I think you were worried about Helen."

He nodded. "Go on," he said.

"You said you thought she wasn't happy—up there. You said, or I thought you said, that she had only been there two years and she hadn't got used to it."

"That surprised you?"

"In one way, very much. I had assumed—I don't know why one does assume these things, but I assumed you'd been married some time. What you said seemed to imply that the marriage was fairly recent. It was that that surprised me."

"Not her being unhappy?"

"It was you who said she was unhappy."

"Don't you think she is?"

I got up and went to the locker for more beer. "Look, Cyril," I said, "is this any business of mine?"

"You mean it's no business of mine to ask you?"

I refilled both our glasses. "I think that's up to you," I said. "Whether I am qualified to give you any sort of an answer is a different matter."

"All right. I do ask, nevertheless."

"For what my opinion is worth," I said, "I don't think she's unhappy. On the other hand, I don't think she's particularly happy. I get the impression that she's in some way—I don't know, unsettled, undecided. As if she was waiting for something to happen."

He nodded but said nothing.

"Since it's arisen," I said, "is the marriage in fact fairly recent?"

"We've been married two years," he said. "Her father died very suddenly and she was left very much on her own. She seemed to feel that very much, being on her own like that. She'd been married before. They were friends of mine, she and her father. I—I offered her a home." He drank again and put his glass down with the same elaborate care. He lifted a face that was almost comical in its woefulness. He said, "Wouldn't you have done the same?"

I thought, Damn the man, he's no right to do this to me, me of all people. I said, "Were they town people? Perhaps the place—"

"Oh no," he said. "No, they lived just up the river here. Just as quiet a place as mine."

For a moment I think I almost gaped at him. But I had to be

certain. I said, "Not that old stone house right down on the bank? I saw it the other day from the river and wondered whose it was."

"That's right. An old farm, only there's no land with it now. Nice old place, but very isolated. More than mine, really. Casson was the name. Their name, I mean. The house is called Herons."

Casson, I thought, and then I remembered. The man with the gun, Jack's master, used to work for Mr. Casson, but Mr. Casson had died a few years back, and they hadn't decided what they wanted done with the place. And Helen Tomlinson had been Helen Casson. Originally, that is. She had been Helen something else before she had become Helen Tomlinson. I was still trying to work out the implications of this when I realised that Cyril was watching me, waiting for a reply. He would be, of course. I jerked my mind back to the course of the conversation. What I said just about made sense, but only just. I said, "It wouldn't catch the wind the way yours does."

"The wind?" he said. "No, no, it's a lot more sheltered. But—"

"You said Helen didn't like a wind. It does get on some people's nerves, you know. If she had grown up in a sheltered corner like Herons, it might take some getting used to."

"She didn't," he said. He seemed sunk in dejection again.

"Didn't what?"

"Didn't grow up there. Charles Casson bought Herons—I don't know, some years back, but he was alone then. Helen was —I suppose she was with her first husband. Anyway, she wasn't there. I didn't even know he had a daughter. Then he said he had a widowed daughter coming to join him from up in the north somewhere, and the next time I went out to see him, there she was. She was Mrs. Harper then. Very quiet and very sad. Well—she's still very quiet. You'll have noticed that. Doesn't say much. Then she hadn't been there more than a couple of years when Charles died. Great strong chap he was, too. It was the river did for him, really. He got caught out in a storm when he was fishing, and the tide left him. He knew too much to try to walk home. He had to sit it out till the tide came in again. The next day he was down with pneumonia, and the day after it was all over. So there she was, alone again. She hasn't had much luck. I was—I was fond of her, of course, by then. So I—well, you can see how it was. Only I don't know really if it was the right thing. You said you felt she was restless. Well, that's it. She doesn't say so, of course. Only I don't think she's ever really settled down."

I said, "I'm sorry." There didn't seem anything else I could say. I was sorry, too. Sorry for poor, kind Cyril and sorry for Helen, and sorry over the whole damned business, only I still did not know what it was all about.

He said, "That's why—I'm afraid you may think I rather commandeered you, but it's good for her to see people. I mean, people we can make friends with. She doesn't go out, you know —hardly at all."

I tried to find something to say that would not be too nauseatingly hypocritical. I had to say something, if only to reassure him. I said, "My dear chap, it's meant a great deal to me. I'm a bit on my own myself at the moment, to tell the truth."

"Yes," he said. He looked at me. He was very far from being a fool, for all his simplicity. "Yes, I thought you might be." He got up and went and put his head out of the hatch. He stayed there a moment, looking out into the grey daylight. Then he came back. "I didn't mean to burden you with all this," he said. "I'm sorry. I've no right, really. Only I thought I might have blown off steam a bit when I was tight. I do, you know. I get worried, and then it's all apt to come out. So I thought I'd better clear things up, in case."

I said, "It's no burden." I was not quite sure how far this was true. What was true was that I had come, unwittingly, with half the burden already on me. Whether he had lightened it or added to it I really did not know. But already I knew one thing.

There was only one way of finding out. I should have to ask Helen. If Helen belonged to Herons, two things followed. She was involved, somehow and to some extent, with the business that had brought me to Leremouth. And she was not on the same side of the fence as Mr. Matthews, because Mr. Matthews did not know about Herons. I had to speak to her, partly because I had to know and partly because I could not bear to be at cross-purposes with her, as I suspected I was.

Cyril said, "You're not thinking of going just yet?"

"Well—not immediately, perhaps. But I must get on some time."

He nodded. He said, "Put me ashore, will you, like a good chap? I've got things to do in town. But I wanted to clear this up. I'm grateful to you."

I said, "There's nothing to be grateful for."

When he was back on the steps, he said, "Come up and see us, won't you?"

"I will," I said. He lifted a hand and went off along the quay in his quick stride. I backed the pram off and paddled back to *Madge*. I wanted to think.

In particular I wanted to think about Jack's master out at Herons. If he was keeping an eye on the place, he must be Helen's man. That was on the assumption that Helen now owned it. But if she did, why was it left as it was? Here she was, married to Cyril and living up on top of Bonnet Point. Unsettled she might be, but she was hardly likely in any case to go back to Herons. The place could have been cleared and sold long before now, and Jack's master relieved of his responsibility.

I remembered thinking that he might report my visit to the owners. This might now mean Helen. He did not know my name, of course, but he would have described me. My appearance is pretty distinctive, if only because of my size, and from what I had seen, there were not many strangers about. In the evening, when Cyril had mentioned our meeting, Helen had asked where it had happened. I had told her, what was true, that it was down near the harbour, and she had asked no more questions. I did not see why the man should have reported, and reported so quickly, his finding me at the house. I thought he had accepted me as harmless, if only on Jack's evidence. On the other hand, I did not see why a man keeping an eye on an empty house should do it with a gun in his hands, even in a remote place like that. There might be something to shoot—rabbits, perhaps, even rats. But I did not really think so. If he was keeping that sort of watch, ten to one he would report any sort of visitor to his employer. There could not be many, with the house placed as it was. Even if he had not reported it immediately, he might well have done so by now. The thing could not be left as it was. I had to talk to Helen, and I had to talk to her alone.

God knows, I wanted to see her, but I did not like this. I did not, as things were, like the idea of deliberately circumventing Cyril. I was in love with his wife, and she had let me make love to her only last night. But my business with her now was, so far as that went, innocent. Only I had to assume that, whatever the business was, Cyril did not know about it, and if Helen had kept it from him, she had presumably done so deliberately. It was all very odd and uncomfortable, but it had to be done.

It need not, in fact, be very difficult. He had said she practically never went out, and he seemed to go out quite a lot. It only meant making sure he was out, and then going and finding her. He was going to be in town during the morning, but I had to walk up the hill, and that did not give me enough time. The only thing was to walk up at lunchtime, when I thought he would be at home, and then watch the house until he went out again. Meanwhile, I had shopping of my own to do, and I had better go and do it.

I did not see Cyril anywhere in town. I thought that at any time from mid-day onwards I could probably find him in the Anchor, but I did not go there. I did what I had to do and went straight back to the boat. I had some food and waited till half past one. Then I went ashore again and walked straight through the town and on to the road that climbed up through the woods to the top of Bonnet. Once I was on the road, I did not want to be seen by anyone. It was not only Cyril I was thinking of, not now. Up to this morning I had thought that so long as the watchers, if I was being watched, did not know of my interest in Herons, it did not matter how much they knew of my interest in the Tomlinsons' house, or even of my reasons for it. Now, disconcertingly, the position was very different. Even though I had in fact met the Tomlinsons by chance, the connection was there, and might be traced. I had to be careful.

In fact there was no trouble over this. There was very little on the road at that time of day. I do not think more than three cars passed me, and I took care that none of them saw me. I was getting good at this sort of scoutcraft. When I got on to the private road, it was only Cyril I had to worry about, and it was still very early in the afternoon. Before I came in sight of the white gate, I left the road and struck out left-handed through the fields. There were no trees to speak of here, but the banks between the fields gave plenty of cover. I came round in a circle and approached the house from a bit south of east. When there was only one bank between me and the edge of the garden, I climbed it and put my head cautiously over the top. I had what I wanted at once. Cyril's car was standing in the drive at the side of the house. I could just see the top of it over the garden fence. The wind had slackened a lot, but what there was was blowing towards me from the direction of the house. I should hear the car the moment it started. I climbed down until my head was just under the top of the bank. Then I sat down and waited.

CHAPTER 12

THE CAR STARTED UP and went off at about three. I did not see it at all. I thought probably Cyril was alone in it. If he had taken Helen with him, it was frustrating, but no worse. I did not for a moment suppose she had gone off in the car by herself, leaving Cyril behind. I waited, impatiently, but for quite a while. I made myself wait, partly to make sure Cyril did not come back, but mainly because I did not want Helen, if she was there, to think I had been watching for the car to go. It is only in farces that the lover pops in from the garden the moment the husband has left. I did not see the situation as farcical. I did not even want to assume my being cast in the role of lover. I still did not place much reliance on what had happened last night.

I gave it ten minutes. Then I got up and headed southwards, towards the end of the point, until the last field gave way to open cliff and I knew I was clear of the end of the garden. Then I turned in westwards to meet the path that Helen and I had gone down last night. I met it lower down than the place where we had stopped and made love. I walked up it wondering whether I should recognise the place when I came to it. There were patches of grass everywhere between the heather and gorse. The slope here was steep and convex. I could not see far up the path, an I could not see the house at all. Then the path flattened suddenly, and I saw Helen hardly ten yards ahead of me. She was sitting on a grass patch at the side of the path, with her hands clasped round her knees, staring out westwards. She had not seen me. She was completely still.

I went on up the path towards her. I did not in any case make much noise, and with the wind blowing across like that, I did not think she would hear me until I was almost up to her. I did not want to startle her. I stopped a little way down the path and stood there looking at her and willing her to turn and see me. It did not have the slightest effect. Whatever it was she was thinking about, it absorbed her utterly. The mouth was set firm, and I thought the brows were drawn down, as if she was frowning a little. I said, "Helen."

She must have heard me, but the reaction was extraordinarily slow. Her head came round, and for a moment she looked almost through me, as if she could not bring her mind to bear on what her eyes saw. She did not say anything. I walked up and knelt beside her on the grass. I thought this was where we had been last night, but I could not be certain. I said "Helen" again, almost desperately, as if I was trying to wake her out of sleep. She looked at me, steadily and with a concentration I found unnerving. Her face seemed completely expressionless. She said, "What do you want?"

There was nothing hostile or indignant in it. It was a straight question, demanding a straight answer. I said, "I wanted to see you. I've got to talk to you."

"I know that. Why?"

"Because of something Cyril told me this morning."

She frowned and shook her head. "I don't mean that," she said. "I mean why did you come to Leremouth at all? What is it you want me to do?"

I stared at her. I must have been frowning as much as she was. I said, "Helen, we're at cross-purposes somehow. I didn't come to Leremouth to see you. I didn't know you existed. Not when I came here. How could I?"

She looked at me, a long, concentrated, questioning look. She must have come to the conclusion that I was speaking the truth, because some of the suspicion and unhappiness went out of her face. But she remained doubtful and confused. We both were. She shook her head again, as if the thing was too much for her. Then she let her breath go in a long sigh. She said, "But you killed Evan Maxwell, didn't you?"

I suppose, now, this did not surprise me as much as it would have a few hours earlier. I said, "I killed him, yes. I don't know how you know, but I killed him."

She seemed to find this more puzzling than ever. "But the name, of course," she said. "I knew your name. It was in the papers."

"Of course it was. But that was four years ago. Why should you remember it? It wasn't reported much. It wasn't a particularly interesting case."

"It was to me," she said. "He was coming to Leremouth when you killed him."

"I know that. At least, I thought he must have been. But I didn't know it was anything to do with you. Not till this morning. Then I wondered."

She said, "Oh yes. It was me he was coming to see."

"Did it matter? My killing him, I mean?"

"Matter? It mattered enormously."

"Then I'm sorry," I said.

She looked at me with her eyes open. Then for the first time that afternoon she managed the ghost of a smile. "Sorry?" she said. "You really don't understand, do you? You can't. It was the best thing you ever did."

I smiled at her. "Ever?" I said.

She coloured slightly, but still kept her eyes resolutely on mine. She was no longer smiling. She said, "I'm afraid so, yes." She turned her face away then and stared westwards over the sea, as she had when I had first seen her. She said, very quietly, "You still haven't answered my question."

"Which question?"

"Why did you come to Leremouth, if not to find me?"

"Maxwell said something before he died. I won't go into the whole story. But it seemed to mean that he was coming to Leremouth, to a particular place at a particular time. And it seemed to be important. Very important. I thought I'd see if I could find out what it was he was after. When I got here I met Cyril by chance. It was in the pub, the evening I arrived. He asked me up here and I met you. The next thing was that I discovered Herons and came to the conclusion that that was where Maxwell had been heading for. It was only this morning that I found out from Cyril that Herons was your father's house and that you would have been there at the time. You knew I'd been to Herons?"

"Yes. Yes, Fenton told me."

"Fenton being the man I met there—Jack's master?"

She frowned again. She said, "Jack?"

"Fenton has a dog called Jack. A good dog."

She said, "Oh, a dog. Yes, I think he has a dog. But what—" She was mildly puzzled but not interested.

"Never mind," I said. "But I thought at the time that Fenton, if that's his name, might have told the owner about his meeting with me. It was only this morning that I understood that you were the owner. Then I thought I had to come and talk to you."

She thought for a moment, still staring out westwards over the Channel. Then she shook her head again and turned back to me. She said, "Why?"

"Why? Partly because I didn't want you to think what you have been thinking—that I was interested in you only because you were the owner of Herons. I couldn't bear you to think that. Especially after last night."

She turned away again, and spoke without looking at me. She said, "Last night has nothing to do with it."

I said, "But Helen—" I think I put out a hand and touched her arm, but the skin was cold, as if I was touching a statue.

She did not move or turn her head. She said, "What was your other reason?"

I dropped my hand. I was still kneeling beside her, but this seemed suddenly incongruous. I got to my feet, rather stiffly and awkwardly, and stood there looking down at her dark hair and white averted face. I said, "I suppose because I thought you might be able to explain the thing to me—why Maxwell had been coming here, what the whole thing is about."

She said, "I can't do that." For a moment neither of us said anything. Then she said, "Is that all you know—what you've told me?"

I felt a sudden surge of anger and helplessness. "That's all," I said.

She nodded. Then she moved. I think it was the first time since I had seen her that she had moved anything except her head. She loosed her arms from round her knees and got to her feet. Then she turned and stood facing me. The physical attraction was still there, as overpowering as ever, but I felt that the little distance between us had become an unbridgeable gulf. She said, "Will you do something for me?"

"I expect so." My anger had gone, and I felt resigned and hopeless. "What is it you want me to do?"

"Go away from here. Right away. Away from Leremouth altogether. Go away on your boat and never come back. And forget the whole thing. Just as if it had never happened."

"If that's what you want," I said.

I think something of my despair must at last have got through to her. She seemed to relent a little. She put out a hand to me. I tried to take it in mine, but she just touched my fingers and took her hand away. Her fingers were as cold as her arm had been. She said, "That's what I need."

"There's nothing I can do to help you?"

"Only go away."

I could not find anything more to say. I just nodded. I left her standing there and turned and went off down the path towards the end of the point. I do not know whether she stayed there or went back to the house. I did not turn round to see. I went down the path until it ran out in the final jumble of crags that marked the end of the green slope and the top of the vertical rock-face. The sea was not very far below me now. It rolled eastwards before the steady wind, and I heard it, though I could not see it, breaking repetitively on the rocks at the bottom of the cliff. It was not a sea I should choose to go sailing on for fun, but for a thing as stiff as *Madge* it was perfectly manageable and not in the least dangerous. I could not make up my mind to go tonight. But I knew that, unless the weather changed, I must sail in the morning. There was nothing to stop me and nothing more here to keep me. Whatever it was Mr. Matthews and his lot were after, it was Helens secret, not mine. The important thing now was to move on before they connected it with Leremouth at all.

I sat for a bit, looking out over the sea as Helen had been looking out from higher up the cliff. The very fact that I had taken my decision, and that there was only one thing I could do, left nothing between my mind and its unhappiness. It seemed very difficult to believe that less than a fortnight ago I had been quietly but fairly blissfully happy in the mere experience of freedom and an ordinary way of living. Like most of the other people in the world, I had let myself think that this was not enough. I had gone waltzing off after the excitements. I had had my excitements. They had not lasted long. Now I had to start all over again. I thought what I needed was work to do. I would take *Madge* a bit further up the coast. Then I would sell her for what she would fetch, and get back to my car, and set about finding myself a job. In the meantime, there was the evening to get through. I thought it would do no harm to get mildly drunk. In any case, I could not go without saying good-bye to Cyril. Unless I was much mistaken, it should be possible to combine the two objectives. But it would have to be at the Anchor, not at the house on top of the point. I got up and began making my way up the path.

Long before I got near dangerous ground I turned off and made my way along a path between the gorse and heather on the east-facing slope of the point. It was only when I had got well along towards the woods that I turned up into the fields and found my way back to the road.

I joined it not far above the elbow where the trees opened up and you could see the whole length of the estuary up-stream. It had been full flood somewhere about noon, and the tides were getting bigger. There was still nothing much to see between the trees but a great sheet of water, white under a white sky and dappled with the wind. Only under the west bank the water lay dark and motionless almost in the shadow of the trees. It was no longer any concern of mine, but I wondered why Evan Maxwell had had his mind on the high tide. He was coming by road, not by sea, and he was coming to see Helen, or so she said. And Helen was already at Herons, living with her father, with Cyril Tomlinson calling on them and getting fond of the pale widow who seemed so sad and spoke so little. I tried to remember what Cyril had said about Helen's coming to Herons. I knew he had said that she had come from somewhere in the north, and had not been there very long when her father had caught cold out on the river and died of it next day. Then she had married Cyril and gone to live in the house on top of the point. And that was two years ago. It did not look, on this, as if she could have been very long at Herons when Maxwell had set out on his journey to meet her and had met, instead, me and my dog. But she must have been there, and I still did not know where the high tide came into it.

I took a last look at the river and went on down the road. I should never know more about it than I did now, because it was no concern of mine. It was no concern of mine because Helen no longer was. The trouble was that this was not true. I went on down through the dark woods towards the clustered roofs of the town. There was no wind here at all. The streets were quiet and lifeless, and I suddenly hated the whole place. I hated the way it crouched there between the hanging trees and the flat water. It was a sad, furtive place, where sad things happened and nothing ever seemed to get properly explained.

I rowed out to *Madge* and started putting things in order for the morning's sailing. My heart was not in it, but there was nothing else I could do. At half past six I went ashore again and made straight for the Anchor. The first thing I saw was Cyril's back. It was a rounded, rather dejected back that did not show off his nicely cut jacket to the best advantage. He was perched on a stool, leaning forwards over the bar. There was no one else in the place, not even the landlord. As a picture of a man escaping from home, it was not encouraging.

I said, "Hullo, Cyril," as I came up to him from the door. His response was galvanic. I could not help comparing it with Helen's a few hours earlier. He swung round so suddenly that he almost knocked himself off his stool. He reached out an arm to hold me in a clasp like the clasp of a drowning man. He said, "Peter, thank God you've come. This place was giving me the willies. What are you drinking?"

I said, "Whisky, please," and he shouted, "Bert!" and the landlord emerged from a door at the far end of the bar. He gave me a double whisky and the same, without being asked, to Cyril. Cyril paid and the landlord vanished as he had come. We were alone again in the empty bar. I sat on the stool next to him, and we waved our glasses at each other and drank.

He said, "I am glad to see you. I wondered where you'd got to."

I did not think this was enough of a question to demand an answer. I said, "Look, Cyril, this is by way of good-byes. I'm weighing my hook in the morning." To anyone else I should have said merely that I was going, but Cyril liked sea language for its own sake. It had made him a lot of money.

He said, "Oh God, old boy, I'm sorry about that. Must you? You haven't been here long."

"I'm afraid I must, yes. Unless it blows up, of course, but I don't think it's going to."

He looked at me in that curious shy, half-sideways way of his, which was so much less direct than Helen's straight stare, but was almost equally penetrating because of the simplicity behind it. He did not ask me the question he had in his mind. Instead he sighed and said, "Well, if you must, you must. You know your own business best. But we'll miss you." He said "we," not "I." He referred to Helen only once more during the entire conversation, and that was the last thing I ever heard him say. We drank four double whiskies each, not counting what he had had before I came in. I do not know how long we took over it, but it must have been an hour or more. After a bit, others of the regulars came in and joined us, and the conversation became general, though on Cyril's part at least increasingly incoherent. Finally he looked at his watch and slid down off his stool.

"Must be going," he said. He did not, this time, add the bit about catching it. What in fact he dreaded was going home at all—home to the house which I at that moment would have given half I possessed to be able to go to, with or without him. I wondered whether he would suggest my going, but I should have known him better than that. When we got outside into the street, he put a hand on my arm and gave it a squeeze. He said, " 'Bye, Peter." Then he gave me one of his quick sideways looks. "Helen know you're going?" he said.

I looked at him, but I did not catch his eye. He was staring along the street away from me. "I don't think it will surprise her," I said.

He nodded and raised a hand. Then, still without looking at me, he was off. I watched him for a moment, and then went off too. I walked to the pier steps and down to the pram. I was full of unhappiness, but the whisky had done its job. I observed my unhappiness as a phenomenon rather than feeling it where it hurt. I did nothing more to the boat that night. Tomorrow would do for that. I ate a scratch meal and got into my berth before there was any danger of sobering up.

CHAPTER 13

I MUST HAVE BEEN SLEEPING too hot, to dream like that. I think the weather must have changed as soon as it got dark. The wind went almost completely, and it got very airless and close. I had got into my sleeping bag still full of the Anchor's whisky and pulled the bag tight round me. When I finally did wake up, I was sweating and parched with thirst, but before I woke up, I had this dream. I do not know how long it really went on. I think I read somewhere that the dreams you remember all happen in the last few seconds before you wake up, but the theory may be out of date now. I only know that this dream seemed to go on for hours. I dreamed that Cyril had told me he had lost Helen and wanted me to help him find her. I do not think I actually dreamed this part. As you often do, I started the dream knowing that this had happened. The dream itself was all the looking for her. I was looking for her on the sands. I knew that Cyril was somewhere about looking for her, but I had lost him too. It was dark on the sands and I could not see more than a very little way. I had to find her quickly, because the tide was coming in, and if I did not find her, she would be drowned. At last I heard her calling to me. She called, "Peter, Peter." She was calling very quietly, almost in a whisper, but the voice was very close. I knew it must be Helen, because it was Helen I was looking for, but it did not sound like her. The odd thing was that I recognised, in my dream, what I must have heard on the cliff that afternoon but not consciously recognised: that there was something unusual in the way she spoke. I had heard her say so little before that afternoon that the unusual quality, whatever it was, had not come out. During the afternoon it had. I had been too much taken up with what she said to recognise it then, but in my dream I did, and I knew that the voice calling to me was different. I tried to move towards the voice, but I was hampered by the sand, which was soft under me. I struggled desperately to free myself, and woke up struggling in my restricting bag. It was pitch dark.

I knew now that it was only a dream. I pulled the top of the bag open to cool myself and flopped back on to the pillow, almost panting in the closeness of the cabin. Then I heard something which was no part of my dream. I heard the hatch pushed very quietly back, and a second afterwards the voice said "Peter" again, very softly. I groped for the torch I kept hanging above my berth, and while I groped, I heard the hatch go further back and someone starting to climb down into the cabin. I found the torch and switched it on as I rolled over on my side, still in the bag. Celia was standing in the after end of the cabin. She had nothing on but a swim suit, and she was dripping wet. She stared into the torch-beam for a moment. Then she turned and pulled the hatch to over her head. She did it carefully and quietly. When it was all secure, she turned again, reached out a hand and clicked on the overhead light.

I said, "Celia! Where have you come from?" I said it almost in a whisper, because she had whispered to me.

"I'll tell you," she said. "Can I have a towel?"

I climbed out of the bag and found a towel for her. She stood there, drying herself down, and looking at me all the time while I sat on the edge of my berth and looked at her. She got herself dry as far as she could, but suddenly shivered violently. She must be cold, of course, but because I was still over-hot from my sleeping bag, I had not thought of it. I got up and lit the gas stove. Then I opened a locker and got out a towelling wrap I used sometimes after swimming. "Put this on, for God's sake," I said. "And better get those wet things off from under it. I'll make you something hot." I gave her the wrap and went past her to the galley to put the kettle on. When I came back with the tea, she was standing over the stove, bundled in the wrap. The two segments of her swim suit were hanging on the drying string above the top of the stove. I poured out tea for both of us, for her because she was cold and wet, for myself because I was parched from the whisky and the sleeping bag. I sat down on my berth and she came and sat down on her old berth opposite me. "Now tell me," I said.

She said, "I'm not quite sure where to begin."

"Well—start by telling me where you've come from. All right, you've swum from the quay, obviously. Where before that?"

"I've got a room in the town," she said. "I came in by car this evening and took the room. I saw *Madge* in the harbour. I went up to my room and waited till everyone was in and quiet. Then I let myself out and came down. I've left a sweater and slacks on the steps. I've got to get back before anyone knows I've gone. I've left the door unlocked."

I nodded. "Right," I said. "Next—why all this secrecy? I take it you're being watched?"

"I may be. So may you. But I reckon they'll have counted me safe for the night—I mean, if they're here at all. They'll expect me to come down and see you in the morning. That's where I'm going to fool them. I'll come down pretty early, properly dressed, and hail you from the steps. You mustn't answer, do you understand? You mustn't show up at all. They mustn't even see your face in the scuttles. Then I'll go away, as if I'd failed to make contact with you. Then later I'll get the car and drive back up-country again, as if I'd given it up. They can make what they like of that. But they'll have to assume that I haven't got through to you." She drank her tea and put her cup down. "That's if they're here at all," she said. "They may not be, yet. I hope they're not. But I think they will be. The important thing is that I should speak to you first."

"All right so far. Now—who are they? I take it they're the people who hired you. I mean, a fortnight ago, or whenever it was?"

She looked at me very straight. She said, "Yes. I'm sorry, Peter. I didn't know how serious it was. I still don't know what it's all about. But I know it's serious."

"Why you?" I said. "For God's sake, why you, Celia?"

She smiled, but it was a wry smile. "What is a nice girl like you doing in a place like this?" she said. "Do you ever expect a straight answer to that question?"

"I've never had occasion to ask it. But I suppose not."

"Good for you. Don't ask it now, then. Only—only I didn't know it was going to be you. I didn't know you were going to be the person you are. And I found I couldn't leave it like that." She was no longer smiling. She said again, "I'm sorry, Peter."

"Then I'm sorry, too."

"For what?"

"For what happened at Carristowe."

"You don't have to be. I deserved it. Besides—oh, all right, I wanted you, Peter. But not like that. I couldn't stand that. That's why I got out. But I expect you'd have put me out, anyway."

"I don't know," I said. "I missed you. But it's no good going back over all that. Who are these people?"

"I don't really know, of course. They've got quite an organisation. But there are only two of them that count. The rest are just hirelings."

"Who are they, then?"

"I know them as the Smiths. God knows who they really are. Two brothers."

I said, "There was a man I met before you picked me up." I described Mr. Matthews. "Is that one of them?"

She nodded. "It's one of them, yes. But it might be either.

They're both like that. Terribly respectable. But I think probably pretty dangerous, only I didn't know that at the time."

"And you don't know what they're after—with me, I mean—the brothers Smith?"

"I don't know what's behind it all. What they're immediately interested in is your movements. Where you go, what you do. At least, I got the impression that you might at some time be of use to them and they just don't want to let you out of their sight. They knew you were going cruising, and that made it difficult for them."

"And that's where you came in?"

"Yes."

"And what happened when you signed off at Carristowe?"

"I told them—I told them I couldn't go on with it. They can't make me work for them. They've got nothing on me. I got the impression—I don't know, but I think the thing they fastened on was the fact that you suspected something."

"You told them that?"

"I—they questioned me pretty closely. You did, didn't you?"

"Yes, Celia, I did. It made me rather angry. I get angry at times."

She nodded and for the first time looked away from me. We had kept our voices very low, but now she spoke so quietly that I could only just hear what she said. She said, "So they told me. Afterwards. Not all of it before. They wouldn't, of course."

"But you came here all the same?"

"I had to come," she said. "Don't you believe that?"

"I don't think I know what to believe." I thought for a moment. "How did you find me—here, I mean?"

She said quickly, "On my own. I'm not—I haven't been in touch with them since after Carristowe. It wasn't difficult, you know. I knew where about you'd have got to. It was only a matter of looking in the harbour for *Madge*. It's only taken me a couple of days."

"But you think they may have followed you?"

"Not me, you. I think they will have made it their business to know where you are. Have you been here long?"

"Not long. I'm sailing in the morning."

She got up. She said, "Peter, can't you get out of this? Get right away out of it? You've got the boat."

"I was going to, in fact. I'm—I'm no longer interested."

"Please do. I don't know what it's all about, but if it's anything serious, I think these people could be dangerous."

I got up and faced her. "What about you?" I said.

She shrugged. "I'll be all right so long as they don't know I've spoken to you. They wouldn't like that. I must go now." She turned away from me, pulling her arms out of the sleeves of the wrap. I took the tea things back to the galley. I was still rinsing them when she came aft in her swim suit. We did not touch each other at all, not all the time she was on board. She said, "Shall I see you some time?"

I told her my bank address. "You could write to me there," I said. "Let's both think about it."

She nodded. "Now you go back to your berth," she said. "And remember, don't show up at all until—I don't know, say, nine. I'll be gone by then."

"All right." I went back and sat on the berth. She put the light out. It was pitch dark again and absolutely quiet. I heard the hatch slide back and then presently I heard it shut again. I heard nothing else at all, not even sounds in the water. I got back into my sleeping bag because it was the sensible thing to do. I hardly expected to sleep. I found myself wondering, of all things, about the difference between Celia's voice and Helen's. It was not the voice, it was the way of speaking. I had recognised it in my dream, but now that I was awake, I could not put my finger on it. They were very different people, apart from the way they spoke. There was all the difference in the world. I liked Celia, even against the evidence. I could not easily believe there was any real wickedness in her. I loved Helen, but I knew that I could. It did not seem very reasonable. I gave it up. I should sail out of Leremouth in the morning, and I did not think I should ever see either of them again.

I slept very little. When it got light outside, I began looking at my watch and wondering when Celia would come down to the quay and whether I should hear her when she did. I hoped not. Even if you are obeying instructions, there is something very disturbing in hearing someone call to you and not answering. It is a thing you do sometimes in childhood and are haunted by for the rest of your life. The mere denying of yourself to the other person is a monstrous act which cuts at the root of humanity. Even if the other person is an enemy, you are going to feel bad about it afterwards. It it is someone you are fond of, it is like cutting off part of yourself. I could not bear the thought of hearing Celia call, and not answering, and then never seeing her again. It was what she wanted, but it was a wretched way to part with anyone. The last time I looked at my watch, it was much too early to expect her anyway. It was after that that I went properly to sleep.

I woke up with a headache and a sense of inescapable misery. My watch said half past eight. I scrambled out of my bag as if I had overslept and missed an appointment. I knew this was nonsense. I could not even go to the scuttle and look out, because I had promised not to. Not for another half-hour. In any case, there would be nothing to see. Celia had said nine, but she would be away by now, out of Leremouth altogether. I should not see her now, or hear her call. But I must do nothing until nine, or nothing that could be seen from outside the boat. I went aft in the grey light from the scuttles and put the kettle on in the galley. Then I dug out a bottle of aspirins and sat waiting until I had tea to take them with.

It was only then that it occurred to me that there was no wind at all. It was completely still. The boat was so motionless, she might have been in a mud berth. I had been all set to sail out of Leremouth, and now there was no wind to sail with. I could motor down-river and hope to pick up something in the way of a sailing breeze outside, but it would be slow work, especially once the tide started making. Even outside there might be next to no wind, and I might have to motor on up the coast if I did not want to anchor or drift until a wind came up. But I had to go. I had told Helen I would, and now I had told Celia. More than that, if Celia was right, and my movements were in fact being watched, I had stayed in Leremouth quite long enough, and it was time I drew the hunt elsewhere.

I checked the fuel tank. There was enough for most contingencies, but not for a day's motoring, and I knew I had nothing in the cans. I should have to fill the cans before I left. I did not want to go ashore at all. I did not want to be in Leremouth again, not ever. But I had no choice. There was a pump just above the quay. I could take the cans ashore and get them filled and be back on board inside ten minutes.

I drank three cups of tea and swallowed three aspirins with the first. Then I sat about in the grey light, waiting for my headache to stop and waiting for nine o'clock. I thought I still had the headache when my watch at last said nine, but when I had moved about a bit, I found it had gone. I went straight to the scuttle and looked out. There was nothing to look out at that I had not seen plenty of times before. The few boats in the harbour, the quay with one or two people moving on it, the town piled up the side of the hill, very drab in the grey light, and over the town the huge, dark bank of unmoving trees. I could not wait to get away from it now, wind or no wind.

I got dressed and slammed the hatch back. If anyone saw me come up into the cockpit, I did not see them. I got up the empty cans from the fo'c'sle and dropped them into the pram. Then I got in myself, got out rowlocks and oars and cast off from *Madge*. The tide was still well down. There was not much water in the harbour. Under the steps there would be enough to float the pram, but not much more. When I got near the steps, I looked over my shoulder, picking up my line in. I thought there was something just showing in the water under the steps, but I could not see what. I rowed on cautiously until I thought I was almost on top of it. Then I easied and turned round to look.

There was about a foot of water below the steps and Celia's face was six inches under. She must have been just about resting on the bottom. The eyes were wide open and the face chalk white under the greenish water. There was dark hair floating round it. Everything was dead still, so that she might have been in a coffin with a glass lid, but as I looked, the way of the pram set up a ripple in the water, so that the hair stirred a little. Nothing else moved at all. She was fully dressed, not even in jersey and slacks, but with a skirt on and walking shoes on her feet. Properly dressed, as she had said she would be. She had got up early and dressed properly, but someone had been up before her and had been waiting for her.

I looked all round the harbour. From down where I was I could see no one, and as far as I could tell, no one could see me. I backed the pram off, turned her and rowed back to *Madge*.

CHAPTER 14

There was nothing I could do, and they, whoever they were, knew it. I did not think they had left Celia under the steps for my benefit. They could not be certain I should find her, and if there had been anything of a sailing breeze, I should not have. Even though I had in fact gone ashore, someone might well have found her before I did. There were people about on the quay by then, though not many, and someone might have looked down and seen her. I thought she had been left there because that was where she had died and she could not be moved. I could imagine, far too clearly for comfort, what had happened. I imagined Celia coming down early in the morning to an apparently deserted harbour. She would have been conscious of the fact that she might be watched, because that was what the whole manoeuvre was meant for, but I doubted if there was anyone in sight when she reached the quay. I imagined her half-way down the wet, slippery steps, starting to hail *Madge* and then finding that there was, after all, someone at the top of the steps above her. It would not have taken long. There would have been enough water there even then. He would have held her under until the legs had stopped their reflex jerking. Then he would have just left her in the water and walked back up the steps to a deserted harbour. He would have been wet, but probably hardly above the knees, and it might not be very noticeable. All he wanted was the nerve and the strength and a complete absence of pity. Looked at now, her masquerade was unbearably pathetic. It was so useless and conceived in such total ignorance of what she was up against. Her death was useless too, even to those who had killed her, because she had already done what they had killed her to stop her doing.

But I could do nothing. If I tried to make trouble, I knew only too well what would happen. There would be evidence discreetly forthcoming that I knew her, and that she had sailed in *Madge* as far as Carristowe. There would probably be evidence, false in intention but true in fact, that she had been aboard with me here in Leremouth. There would probably be fingerprints of hers, if an expert looked for them, all over the varnished woodwork of the cabin. What hope would a man with my record have in the face of evidence like that? But that was only if I tried to make trouble. If I kept quiet, there would be nothing against me and, ten to one, nothing against anyone. An unfortunate accident, difficult to explain but undeniable. A visitor on an early-morning walk had slipped on the steps and for some reason been unable to save herself. Visitors do these things, just as they get caught on the sands by the rising tide. So I should keep quiet, and get off my moorings and sail as planned, though without as much fuel on board as in these conditions I should have liked. But some time, somehow, I should find Mr. Matthews and his brother Smith, and this time, whatever there had been with Evan Maxwell, there would be no doubt at all about my intentions. I clenched my hands until the nails bit into my palms. I had never been as angry as I was now, but this time my anger had calculation in it. It would keep, and be there when I wanted it. I went to the galley and found the glass with the smear of lipstick still on it. I washed it very thoroughly with detergent, and polished it, and put it back with the rest. Then I set about the business of getting away.

I left the pram in the water on a long tow-rope. I did not even make the gesture of getting sail up. I started the motor and got it running quietly in neutral. When I cast off the mooring, the boat did not move a foot in the glassy water. I put *Madge* slow ahead, came round in a sweep wide enough not to foul the tow-rope and pointed her out between the pier heads. I did it all in the most leisurely fashion. There were, as always, one or two people watching. I did not look at them at all closely, but I saw no face that was even remotely familiar. I cleared the heads and turned down-river against the steady, invisible set of the tide. The way of the boat brought a gentle movement of fresh air on my face, but that was all. In all that huge expanse of grey water and grey sky the boat was the only thing that moved.

When I was well down-river, with nothing to be seen of Leremouth but the south head of the harbour and one line of houses on the side of the hill, I kicked the motor into neutral and throttled right back. The boat came very slowly to a stand-still, holding true on her course all the time because there was nothing to head her off it. She sat there, with the motor turning over quietly in neutral and the ripples of our wake spreading out fainter and fainter across the flat water astern. After a bit even they disappeared, and then there was no movement anywhere, and no sound but the muffled throb of the motor. I hesitated, and then went below and switched it off. I knew, only too well, that I could not in fact leave Leremouth yet. But I had to think.

I had of course to make a show of leaving, as if I had simply been there long enough and was ready to move on. There was always the chance that this might be accepted at its face value. It was still just possible that they had not seen any significance in my stay at Leremouth and still did not know that this was where the answer to their question lay. But I did not think it very likely. Celia, poor Celia, still for all I knew staring up through six inches of green water at the bottom of the harbour steps, was evidence to the contrary. Even quiet-spoken little gentlemen like Mr. Matthews do not commit murder in broad daylight in a public place unless the matter is fairly urgent. They were on to something. And Helen, away in her lonely house on top of the point, did not even know they were there. I wanted nothing better, now, than to be quit of the whole damned business, but I could not leave it like that. I had brought them there. Because I could not leave well alone, I had, after all, given them a part at least of what they wanted. Like Celia, I had not taken them as seriously as they deserved. I still did not know what it was all about, but I knew that Helen was involved, and she must be told.

In the meantime, I could not stay where I was. If anybody was making it their business to see me away from Leremouth, they could still, if they had kept at it long enough, see me. Even at this distance, and without sail up, the fact that a boat was no longer moving would sooner or later become apparent. I must find somewhere out of sight of the harbour and then stop and think what was to be done. For the first time, I was thankful for the flat calm. As long as it lasted, you could park a boat, almost as if she was a car, anywhere where there was enough water under her. I re-started the engine and got under way again. I went as slowly as I could make way against the tide, partly to save fuel, but mainly because I did not want to go farther than I need.

Half a mile or so ahead the cliffs threw out a bit of a spur eastwards. I did not know what there was beyond it, but there must be another mile at least to the southern end of the point. I thought if I hugged the spur and then turned in under the cliffs beyond it, I should be finally out of sight of the harbour, and probably out of sight of anyone on land, except presumably an observer right over the cliffs on the eastern face of the point. I crept in cautiously towards the black rocks at the end of the spur. The glassy water reflected the cliff in fantastic detail, but it was impossible to see what was under the surface, and I dared not go in too close. The nearer I got to the end of the spur, the more the line of the cliff south of it moved out to meet it. I began to think that on its southern side there was no eastward projection at all, but merely an obtuse angle in the southward line of the cliff. It was not until I was almost round the outlying rocks that I saw the cove.

It opened with unbelievable suddenness. At one moment all I saw was the unbroken cliff face stretching away to the southern tip of Bonnet. At the next I had swung the bows to starboard and was heading due west right into the flank of the point. First on one side and then on the other the black cliffs towered over me. Ahead, a green cleft opened in the rock and dropped to within thirty or forty feet of the high-water mark. At low tide I reckoned there might be a strip of sand below the rock. I cut the motor and the boat lost way at once. The suddenness of the manoeuvre had taken me by surprise, but in fact *Madge* drifted to a halt at just about the point I should have chosen. I ran forward to clear the anchor and cable. The boat had so little inclination to move that when I had got the anchor down and paid out what I thought was enough cable, I gave the screw a few turns ahead again to carry her to the end of her cable and give the anchor a chance to bite. Then I shut off the motor and sat there, in the utter silence, taking stock.

It was the classic smuggler's cove. At the right state of the tide and in almost anything but a dead easterly, you could get right in and land anything from a keg of brandy to a dozen shivering Pakistanis. I could also think of other uses for the small, utterly secluded sand beach which ought to be there at low tide. But as far as I could tell, no one used it now for anything. I felt sure I could find my way up the rock-face to the bottom of the cleft and from there to the top of the cliff. But there was no sign of steps cut in the rock or any path on the cliff above it. Now that I came to consider it, I saw that, even in high summer, the sun would not touch the head of the cove much after mid-day. What with that and the fact that only full low water would uncover the sand, I could see that it was not, perhaps, after all the ideal picnic beach I had at first thought it. Nevertheless, as a bathing cove at pretty well any state of the tide the thing was perfect, and I thought the local boys must be sadly unadventurous if they had not discovered it.

More to the point, it was the ideal anchorage. I could give *Madge* all the cable she wanted for any state of the tide, and there was still room for her to swing all round her anchor without getting into trouble. When the wind came back, as it must do sooner or later, she would be sheltered from every quarter at all likely, at this time of the year, to produce anything of a blow. As I have said, only a dead easterly, with the seas breaking right into the cove, could worry her. Even then, with a firm sand bottom, there was no reason, short of a gale, why she should drag her anchor. I had my base. As far as I could tell, I was invisible except from out in the river mouth and up on the cliff overhead. Even from the river the cove was not conspicuous. I certainly had not noticed it when I came in. Yet once I was on the cliff, I could not be more than half an hour's scramble from the Tomlinsons' house. I pulled the pram in on its tow-rope and made it fast by its own painter. Then I went below to get myself some food. As soon as I had eaten, I would go ashore and look for a way up the cliff.

In these conditions the cove seemed the quietest place I had ever been in. I tiptoed about the boat and put things down with exaggerated care so as not to break the enormous silence. On three sides the cliffs hung over the glassy water and the unmoving boat. I found myself looking up at them, watching for something to move. I knew there was a path of a sort along the top of the cliff on this side of the point. I had used it myself only the day before. What I could not tell, from down here, was whether or not *Madge* would be visible to anyone on the path. In general, the convex curve of the slope and the vertical rock drop below it would certainly hide a fairly wide stretch of water at the foot of the cliff. But here the slope was broken by the cleft running down to the head of the cove, and it might be that at one particular point, where the path crossed the line of the cleft, anyone walking along the path might get a glimpse of the cove and the boat moored in it. That is, if they happened to look down at the right moment. It would probably be quite easy to miss. The only way to settle it was to go up on to the path myself, and this I intended to do. I must not, clearly, try to get near the Tomlinsons' house until after dark, but to reconnoitre this end of the route by daylight was an obvious necessity.

When I was ready, I put on rubber shoes, dropped a fifteen-fathom coil of nylon line into the pram and rowed to the head of the cove. I took up the nylon coil and stepped out on to the rocks. I let the pram go to the end of its painter. I reckoned the tide would be falling from about now on, and I had to give it line to spare. I did not intend, this time, to be away long, but you never knew. I should have to make it fast somewhere up above high-water mark. If the painter was not long enough, I could use some of the nylon line. There was a rubber fender all round the gunwale, and in these conditions the pram would not hurt itself even if it did nuzzle the rock a bit. I tied the painter to one end of the nylon line and slung the coil over my shoulder. Then I started to look for a way up the rock.

It was not in fact particularly difficult. There was only one place where the rock overhung a bit, and even there there were plenty of holds. The strata ran horizontally, and there were shelves and ridges everywhere where the sea had eaten away the softer layers. It would not be so nice coming down, but then I expected to have a fixed line to help me. I was not quite at the top when I ran out of painter. I payed out a couple of fathoms of line and went on climbing. When I got to the top, there was still a loop of loose line behind me, and enough left in the coil to drop a line down to the beach. All I wanted was somewhere to fix it. The best I could do was a spike of rock that jutted out of the slope. It looked firmly anchored, but in a cliff slope like this you never really know what is firm and what is not. I threw a couple of bends round it and then, standing above it, threw my weight backwards against the slope. It did not stir, and I should have to hope for the best. It was only there for an extra hold. With any luck I should not have to swing on it. In any case, it was the best I could do. I made the line fast round it, leaving plenty of slack in the end that joined the painter. Then I threw the running end down to the beach. There seemed plenty to spare. My way back looked reasonably secure, and I started up the slope.

It was scrambling work, energetic but not requiring any thought. I could not see very far above me. The slope must be more convex than I had thought, even here in the cleft, which was all to the good. When I was well up, I came suddenly over the shoulder, and a big stretch of cliff opened up above me. There was gorse and rough grass on it. From what I could remember, I thought I must be pretty close to the path. I flopped down to get my breath back, and at the same moment saw someone on the cliff a hundred yards or so north of me. I wriggled forwards a yard or two and lay flat under a gorse bush. I did not think he could have seen me. I gave it a few seconds and then put my head up very cautiously for a quick look. He was nearer now, and coming steadily my way. He must be on the path, and from the look of it was going to pass ten or fifteen yards above me. I did not have time to take in any details. It was a man, dressed in something dark and walking steadily. He did not seem to be doing anything particular except walking. I got my head down again and looked behind me down the slope. I could see nothing of *Madge* from where I lay, but his head would be a dozen feet higher than mine was. I reckoned I should know soon enough whether you could see her from the path. But perhaps he was not interested in boats. In any case, I could do nothing but wait. I thought if I heard him start to come down the slope towards me, it would be time to get on my feet, but not till then.

In point of fact, I never heard him at all. I waited for what seemed a very long time. I did not find this at all enjoyable. Finally there was nothing for it, and I put my head up again. He was past me, still going steadily, twenty yards southwards along the path. I never saw his face, and there was still nothing about him I could pick on at all. I lay back and let my stomach settle. When next I looked, he was nowhere in sight. The path must have carried him round the curve of the point. I was still not risking more than I could help. I crawled on my hands and knees up to the path and looked down the cleft from there. Still no *Madge*. There was only one thing left to do. I got to my feet, looked long and hard down the slope and then dropped again. I knew what I had seen, because I was looking for it, but I did not think anyone else would have seen it. I had seen the truck of *Madge*'s mast, just showing in the bottom of the green dip. It was quite steady. It would not catch the eye. In any case, the man had not stopped. I had to be content with that. I crawled down the way I had come, and then, when I was over the shoulder of the slope, went down the cleft as fast as I could make it.

CHAPTER 15

THE SKY HAD CLEARED after sunset, and by the time I got to the edge of the garden it was bright moonlight. The air was moving again, blowing in very gently from the west. It was a lovely night, only in the circumstances I could have done without the moon. I had taken twice as long as I had expected coming up the cliff. I did not think there would be anyone walking on the path at this hour, but if there was, I had to make sure that I saw him before he saw me. It was after half past ten when I put my head over the wall and looked at the house. I saw with relief that there were still lights on. If you are not expected, it is not in any case easy to attract the attention of one person in a house at night without being heard by the others. If everyone is asleep, it is very difficult indeed, especially if you are not sure where everyone sleeps. But Cyril was still in his study, or at least the lights were still on there, and there were lights at the other end of the house, where I thought Helen might be. I worked my way round to the front, where two of Cyril's windows were uncurtained. He was there all right, sitting at his work-table. He was not writing. He did not seem to be doing anything but sitting there, staring out of a window he could not see through because, even with this moon, it was much lighter inside than it was out. I was reminded at once of the picture I had had of him in the Anchor bar. There was the same dejected droop of the shoulders and general air of listlessness. He looked now, as he had looked then, like a man taking deliberate refuge in solitude, but finding it, even so, barely tolerable. I felt dreadfully sorry for him. I knew I had only to go and tap at the window and he would welcome me ecstatically, as relief almost beyond hope. But my business was not with him. Whatever his discontents, he must find his own way out of them. I went on along the western side of the house. There was a light in the small room next to the hall, which I thought was Helen's bedroom, but the curtains were drawn. There was still light in the kitchen at the back. The windows were uncurtained, but there was no one there. There was only one more lit window, a small one half-way along the side of the house. This too was curtained. From the steam on the inside of the glass and the plumbing on the outside wall, I took it to be a bathroom. The picture was clear enough. Helen was in the bathroom and on her way to bed. I did not know what Cyril's movements would be. From the looks of him, he might be there for hours. I did not think he would make a move until Helen was in bed, but I could not be certain of this. On the other hand, you cannot tap at a bathroom window when someone is in the bath and expect them to take it calmly. I thought that the only thing to do was to wait until the bathroom light went out and then assume, if I could not see her anywhere else, that she was in her bedroom. At least I was in the shadow of the house here. It was as good a place to wait as any. Then the bathroom curtains were flung back and the casement window half opened to the air.

A small waft of warm, scented steam drifted past me. The panes were still clouded with steam, but through the chink of open window I could see Helen standing just inside. She was naked. I still think it was the most wonderful body I have ever seen. Aesthetically it could no doubt be faulted, but it made aesthetics gloriously irrelevant. I felt hollow and breathless with straight physical desire, but this was not what I had come about. She turned and walked to the door, where there was a wrap of some sort hanging on a hook. She put it on and then came back towards the window. It was now or never. I said, "Helen" in a desperate whisper, and then went right up to the window and whispered "Helen" again.

She opened the window wide, and for a moment we stood looking at each other through it. The light was on my face. She said, "What do you want?" She said it exactly as she had on the cliff. It was only the afternoon before. It seemed an age ago.

I said, "I must see you. There's something I've got to tell you. Something's happened."

She hardly hesitated at all. She said, "Go down on to the cliff and wait. I'll come when I can." Then she turned and went to the door. She switched off the light and went out, shutting the door behind her. I turned back into the moonlight. I was still in a fever of longing and unhappiness, but I knew that this was out of place and almost certainly, to her, unimportant. Cyril had not moved. I went out of the garden and down the path towards the end of the point. When I was out of sight of the house, I sat down to wait. I sat facing the sea. I knew that Helen would come from up the path behind me, and still felt a need to keep a look-out in the other direction, in case there was anyone about on the cliff. I saw nothing but the dark curve of the point and the vast glittering levels of the sea. I heard nothing at all, but suddenly Helen was there, sitting beside me. Her hair was hanging loose, and she was bundled from neck to ankle in something dark. "Now tell me," she said.

I told her everything that had happened from my meeting with Mr. Matthews to my discovery of Celia's body under the harbour steps that morning. I did not, in fact, tell her quite everything. I did not tell her what had happened in Carristowe harbour. She heard me out in silence, sitting there with her hands clasped round her knees and her head bowed slightly forwards. When I stopped, she said, "Why didn't you tell me this before?"

"I didn't think it was necessary. Some of it I didn't know."

"Until this girl came back and told you?"

"Yes."

"Was she in love with you?"

"I don't think so."

"But you made love to her?"

"I think—I think I pretty well raped her. That was when I thought she was spying on me. I got angry."

"And now she's dead. Cyril heard a girl had been drowned in the harbour. A visitor, he said."

"That would be the story."

"You're certain these people are in Leremouth now?"

"I think so, yes."

"Do they know you're here—I mean, up here, now?"

"No. I don't think they can. I've come straight up the cliff. The boat's in a cove under the eastern side of the point. You can't see her except from the sea."

"Do they know you've been coming up here?"

"They could easily find out if they asked a few questions."

"What about Herons?"

I considered this. "I don't think they can know I went there. No one can, except you and Fenton."

For what seemed minutes she said nothing. She sat there, still with her head drooped over her knees. Even in the moonlight I could see the concentration of thought in her face. Then she straightened up and shrugged. It was a curiously un-English gesture. She said, "You said yesterday you would do anything to help me. Will you?"

"What do you want me to do?"

"Get me away from here."

"You mean—?"

"In your boat. To France."

I said, "What about Cyril?"

"Cyril?" She looked at me as if she could not see the sense of this. "You needn't worry about Cyril. He'll be relieved as much as anything."

I thought of that drooping figure in the Anchor bar and in the work-room up at the house. I said, "Perhaps you're right." I thought for a moment. "I make two conditions," I said.

"What are they?"

"First that you understand that there may be an element of risk. The boat isn't an ocean cruiser and I'm not all that of a seaman. So long as the weather holds, we should manage to hit the coast of France somewhere without much trouble. But it might blow up at any time. Do you mind where we fetch up?"

"Not much. I accept that. What's your other condition?"

"I must know what it's all about. There's been murder done. I'm not taking any further hand in the thing unless I know more what's at stake."

She gave me a long hard stare in the moonlight. Then she said, "I'll tell you everything up to one last point. That is because I believe I can trust you up to that point. Beyond that point I wouldn't trust anyone."

"Thank you for the limited compliment, anyway. All right. Tell me as far as you can."

"Now?"

"Why not now? It seems as good a time as any."

She nodded. She said, "My father had a very large amount of money. It was hidden. It still is. He had, I suppose, no right to it. But nor had anyone else."

"This was at Herons?"

"In France. My father was never at Herons. Charles Casson wasn't my father. He was a friend of my father's. A very old friend. My father was French. I'm French."

I said, "That's it!"

"What?"

"Your voice. The way you speak. I knew there was something, but I couldn't put a finger on it. Your English is perfect, but not native English."

"Of course," she said. "I know."

"That's why you never say more than you need?"

"I suppose so. I got into the way of it when I first came over here. Now it's a habit."

I said, "Go on."

"It was at the end of the war. These things happened then. You know that. I was only a child then, of course. The money was in gold. English sovereigns. Beautiful things. Have you ever seen one? It got—it just got left in his hands. The Allies landed and everything was in confusion. He did not have to account for it. He hid it and just waited. He waited a long time. Then I think he started to use it. A little at a time. Very carefully, of course. But perhaps not carefully enough. He had used only a very little of it when these people came to see him. These Englishmen. That was about five years ago."

"Who were they?"

"God knows. Your friend Evan Maxwell and your friend Mr. Matthews and his brother. They came and spoke to my father and then they went away again. I think they gave him time to make up his mind. Or perhaps he agreed, but put them off. I don't know. But they told him that if he didn't pay up, they'd come and take me. I was his weak spot, you see. My mother was dead and he could look after himself. He could look after himself very well, but he was afraid for me. So he decided to send me to Charles Casson. But things went wrong."

"What happened?"

"There was a man we had working for us. He had been with my father in the Resistance. He trusted him. This man—Jean Paul, his name was—didn't know about the money. At least, he didn't know where it was. But he knew all about the plan to get me to England. I think he made the arrangements. And he must have been got at by the Englishmen. Or perhaps just by Maxwell. I don't know what happened, but my father found out about it, and there was a fight. They both used knives. My father killed him, but he was very badly wounded himself. When he—when he knew that he was dying, he told me I must go to England, to Charles Casson. It had all been arranged. And then before he died, he told me where the money was. He wanted me to have it, if possible. But also he wanted to make sure that if they ever got hold of me, I could tell them at once, so that they would not try to make me tell them what I did not know. That makes sense, I think?"

"Of a sort," I said. "Go on."

"When my father was dead, I came here, to Charles Casson. I told you, it had all been arranged. The boatman knew nothing. He was a regular smuggler, and he'd been well paid. But I think Jean Paul had already got word through about my coming over. He must have. It had all been arranged well in advance, because of the tides. But he must have told only Evan Maxwell, and Maxwell decided to double-cross the others and come and get me on his own. And then you killed him, you and your dog. That left nobody who knew. I saw about Maxwell's death and your trial. I knew where he had been coming, of course. He had been coming to meet me at Herons when I landed. He had to. That was the one fixed point. The one certain thing was when I should land at Herons, because of the high tide. You've seen that for yourself. I didn't know he hadn't told the others, of course. After his death, I waited, there at Herons, but no one came. Then I knew. But I've been waiting, more or less, ever since."

"And when Charles Casson died, you married Cyril?"

She nodded. "He wanted me to. He was—he's a kind man. And it gave me a British passport. It seemed the safest thing to do. I could wait here as safely as at Herons."

"Wait for what?"

"The money." She was quite matter-of-fact about it. "When it seemed safe to get it. Now I suppose I'll have to start waiting all over again. And then only if I can get away."

I thought for a moment. Then I said, "Do these people know you by sight?"

"Those two, of course. The one you call Mr. Matthews and his brother. I was there when they came to see my father. That's only five years ago. I haven't changed much. If once they think I'm in these parts, they can look for me until they find me. That's why I've got to go."

"You can manage in France on your own?"

"Of course. It's my country. I know people there. I can arrange things."

"All right," I said. "You want me to land you in France and then leave you?"

She looked at me for the first time with a shade of doubt, but then she nodded. "I think that would be best," she said.

"That's where your trust runs out?"

"Not really. Even if you knew where I was going, you couldn't find the money. No one could find it unless I told them where to look. I trust you with everything but that. I know you'd never be able to force it out of me. You haven't got it in you to do it. You can be violent, but you're not cruel. These people would do anything. My father knew that."

I thought of the quiet, precise Mr. Matthews and Celia down under the water in the harbour. "I think you're right," I said. "You wouldn't consider just telling them where it is and letting them take it?"

She did not say anything. She looked at me sharply, as if she was not quite sure whether I was serious. Then she set her lips tight and shook her head.

"All right. Now—can you get down to the cove where the boat is?"

"What does it involve?"

"A scramble down the cliff and then a climb of forty feet or so down straight rock. It isn't particularly difficult, and there's a rope."

"I'm afraid not. I'm sorry. I can't manage heights. I can't even go up a ladder. You know what it is. It's not a thing one can argue about. It's a simple disability like blindness."

"That I know. If you're like that, I wouldn't touch it."

"Could you take me from Herons?"

"Herons? It seems a very long way round."

She said, "I think it might be best. I've got to go there in any case before I leave. There's something I left there I shall want. And you say they don't know about it."

"I said I didn't think they could know I'd been there. Once they're interested in Mrs. Tomlinson, I suppose they could get back to Herons."

"But could you manage it?"

I thought about this. I said, "I'm not bringing the boat in, for a start. For one thing, she'd be seen. For another, she draws too much water. With a very big tide and split-second timing it might just be done, but the risk of going aground is enormous. That means the pram. I've got no power for the pram. It means rowing with the tide. Not impossible and certainly quiet, but still difficult to get the timing right. What about Fenton?"

"He can be trusted. He was Charles Casson's man. He was there when I came. He's been on the look-out for intruders more or less ever since, just as I have."

"Yes. Yes, he had a gun when I saw him. I thought it was a bit unusual."

"He thought you were all right."

"Not him, his dog. He didn't dare differ."

She looked at me blankly, as she had once before. She said, "His dog?"

I said, "Never mind. Look. Could Fenton hide me and the pram for—I'm not sure, twenty-four hours, I think? It's a very light boat. He and I could carry it anywhere between us."

"Yes, I think so. There are plenty of buildings. And the house itself. Why?"

"I was thinking on these lines. We assume they're watching me. We have to assume they haven't yet identified you. If I'm going to get you off without their knowing it, I've got to lose them, even if only temporarily, before I pick you up. So I thought if I took the pram up to Herons on the night flood, I could lie low there until the next night. They wouldn't see me go up. Even with this moon, you'd have to be keeping a very sharp watch to see a thing of that size go up on the flood. And there's no reason why they should be watching the river at all. Then you could come to Herons whenever it suited you next day, or even early the next night, pick up what you wanted and wait for the night flood. As soon as it was up, we'd put the pram on the water and get out into mid-stream. That would be you and me, this time. The ebb would take us down-river. We could get aboard *Madge* and be away well before daylight."

"The pram can take the two of us?"

"Oh yes, in any reasonable conditions. She's light, but very buoyant, even with two up. They capsize easily, but that only means that you've got to sit still. We'd be wearing life-jackets, of course."

"What would your reasonable conditions be?"

"So long as the wind stays west of south, roughly. We'd be under the lee of the point all the way."

For a moment or two she looked out over the sea, frowning, as I had seen her frown before, in a concentration of thought. Then she turned back to me. She said, "Can you go up tonight?"

I looked at my watch. "I could try," I said. "High water's about 1:30. Even if I don't get to Herons tonight, I can get well up-river and lie up till tomorrow afternoon. It oughtn't to matter doing the last bit by daylight if I have to. But I hope I can make Herons tonight if I hurry. What about Fenton?"

"I'll phone him."

"And you can get there yourself?"

"Yes, yes. Tomorrow evening. You're sure it will be all right?"

"Nautically, yes. I can't answer for the rest."

"All right." We were both on our feet, facing each other. She said, "You'd better go now." Her eyes looked very big and dark in her white moonlit face.

"I'm going," I said. There was nothing else to say and nothing else to do. I went off along the cliff, going hard to get myself out on the water before I lost too much tide and had too much time to think.

CHAPTER 16

I SUPPOSE I should have left the line where it was, but I could not bring myself to do it. There was no question of concealment in it. If anyone had got down the cliff that far, they would know the boat was there anyhow. I told myself that I did not want to make it easy for anyone to get down to the cove while I was away up-river. The truth is, I could not bear to leave fifteen fathom of good line where I could never come back and get it. There was plenty of line on board, but you never know when a particular piece may not turn out to be lethally irreplaceable. I untied it and looped it round the rock. So long as I put an even strain on both ends together, it would still do what I wanted, and when I was at the bottom I could just pull it in.

In fact I hardly needed it. I had been up the rock-face twice and down it once since mid-day, and there was enough light to see what I was doing. There was plenty of water in the cove already, and the pram was floating against the bottom of the rock with most of the painter and underwater. I stepped straight into it, pulled the painter inboard and untied it from the end of the nylon line. Then I let one end of the line go and began pulling the other in. For a moment both ends stood taut against the rock. Then it gave so suddenly that I thought I had brought some of the cliff down on my head, but in fact nothing moved but the line. The running end whipped up the rock like a snake going home, and a moment later the whole lot came slithering down and fell all over the boat. I gathered it into a heap and paddled out to *Madge*.

Time was everything now. I made the pram fast and scrambled on board, pulling the jumble of line after me. I dropped it as it was on the floor of the cockpit. There would be time enough to get shipshape when we were safe back on board again, and that would not be until the small hours of the day after tomorrow. I looked at the anchor cable, but that was no more than a propitiatory gesture. So long as the weather held and no one interfered with her, *Madge* would still be there when we got back. I went below and put on a life-jacket under my guernsey. I took a torch and a spare life-jacket for Helen. I tried to think if there was anything else I ought to take, but I could not see there was. It would be up to Fenton to feed me. I got back into the pram, wrapped the torch in the spare life-jacket and bundled it under the sternsheets. Then I cast off, coiled the painter down carefully in the bows and paddled out into open water.

I headed straight out eastwards. What I could do with the oars was negligible. It was the tide that would get me to Herons if anything did, and the sooner I was out in the full run of it, the better. The water was smooth under the lee of the cliff, but after a bit I felt the breeze on my face and the pram began bobbing about a bit as the tide came under it. Then I turned north and began to row steadily up into the river. I caught a last glimpse of *Madge*, very quiet and white in the moonlight against the dark of the cove. Then, almost as I looked at her, the end of the spur blotted her out as smoothly as if someone had pulled a curtain across. It was a whale of a tide and I was moving fast. All I had to worry about now was holding a course well out in the middle of the river, where I should get all the tide there was and be as far as possible from the harbour as I went past. I began to think the thing was easy. I went on rowing steadily, but I was not going to tire myself.

It was a spectacular night. The moon was nearly full now, with a few wisps of light cloud blowing gently across it. The dark mass of Bonnet towered on my right hand. If I looked over my shoulder, I could see the faint harbour lights of Leremouth still well away ahead of the boat. Everything else, as far as I could see, was a glittering expanse of spangled water. I found myself suddenly free to think, and the thing I thought about was Helen.

I no longer thought of her as the silent woman. I had now, on the face of it, the explanation of her silence, but it was not a complete explanation. I did not think she would be much more forthcoming in French than she was in English. The formidable quality in her remained. She was a woman who made her own decisions and kept quiet about them. If she could not override the opposition, she would go round or through it. When she gave way, she surrendered only to herself. It followed that any relation you had with her would be on her own terms, because that was the sort of person she was, and you took her like that or not at all. I did not see the harm in this, so long as you knew where you were with it. I wanted her on any terms I could get. From tomorrow night I should have her to myself until we got to France. After that it would be for her to decide. I believed she might decide to keep me if she found she could trust me. I had my uses. Beyond that I did not flatter myself. But I wanted her. I wanted her desperately.

The next time I looked over my shoulder I found the harbour lights alarmingly close. Not only close ahead, but close in on the port beam. I had not realised how much the stream turned in westwards at the mouth of the estuary. That of course was where the deep channel lay, which was why the harbour was where it was. I wondered how much the pram, moving with the tide, would show up to anyone looking out from the harbour. Not much, obviously. The fact remained that when I had pictured it in my mind's eye, I had thought of it as much farther out.

A quarter of a mile or so below the harbour mouth I shipped the oars, got off my thwart and settled myself in the bottom of the boat. I even took the rowlocks out of their sockets and let them hang by their strings inside the boat, in case a movement of the polished metal should catch the moon. With only my head above the level of the gunwales and the boat turned broadside to the stream, we drifted past the harbour mouth perhaps a hundred yards out. Apart from the fixed lights on the pier heads, there were very few lights anywhere ashore. One or two of the houses up the hill still had a window lit, but the street lights seemed to be out, as if the Council was taking advantage of the full moon to save a bit on its electricity bills. The whole place seemed somehow smothered in the moonlight. It was difficult to believe, from out here, that there was anyone alive there at all. If there was, I could not see them, and I hoped they could not see me. I lay low until the edge of the trees had covered everything but the pier-head lights. Then I got up on my thwart and started rowing again. I hoped I had not wasted too much time.

From now on I put the work on. I was determined to get to Herons on this flood if it could possibly be done. I had been carefully reassuring about it to Helen, but I did not really think that to complete the journey in the glare of the early afternoon would be very wise. Apart from that, I was, to say the least of it, ill-equipped to lie up for the night in the woods. On the other hand, I did not think it would be safe to complete the journey on foot, leaving the pram somewhere under the bank, and come back for it tomorrow. There was no middle course. Either I reached Herons while there was still enough water under the steps to float the pram, or I settled for a dispiriting and hungry twelve hours somewhere on the river bank. I pushed the light, unhandy craft along as fast as I could, edging always in towards the west bank. Once I was over the flats, I did not think the stream varied much in different parts of the river. The one thing I could not risk was being left high and dry out in the middle.

After a bit I easied and pulled off my guernsey. My life-jacket was of the waistcoat type, with a double skin and an air-trap in between. Worn on the outside, they make little difference to your warmth, but put them under something and they provide a pocket of insulation all round the body. I did not really think I needed to wear it at all up here in the estuary, but I could not quite make up my mind to take it off. I dropped the guernsey on the coiled painter behind me and set off rowing again, glad of the cool air round my arms and neck. When I finally let myself look at my watch, it was just before one. High water was not, theoretically, for another half-hour, but with a tide as big as this one, I reckoned the estuary would fill early. After that, although the level of the water would go on rising, there would be little or no lateral movement. The tide had done me very well, but it had done all it was going to do for me. From now on it was all rowing in slack water, and I did not have more than half an hour left. Once the ebb started, it would go out like water down a drain.

I was clear of the woods now, working my way along under the fields that lay between them and Herons. I thought I knew where the house was, but even when I let myself look over my shoulder, there was nothing to see. I crept past a projecting spit, turned for a look ahead and when I turned back found myself almost opposite the spit again. Here at least the flow was already down-stream, and it was still five minutes before scheduled high water. I pulled doggedly and began to go away from the spit again. I do not know how long this went on, but when next I turned for a look round, there was a light shining almost down on the water and not more than twenty yards ahead. I turned in towards it and after another ten strokes found myself under the wall. Fenton had doused his light now, but I could just see him standing on the steps. The shade of the garden trees was everywhere. Above him, half-way up the steps, a darker shadow vibrated silently. Jack had had his orders and would not bark tonight.

Fenton said, "You made it, then. Tide's just on the turn."

I held on to the bottom of the steps. I was very glad to be able to stop rowing. I said, "It shouldn't be yet, not by rights."

He leant down and took the painter out of the bows. "Always this way at the springs," he said. "Comes and goes very quickly. It's a big tide. Be even bigger tomorrow night. You got anything in the boat?"

I took the spare life-jacket from under the sternsheets and unwrapped the torch. I handed the jacket up to him and shone the torch for a moment down into the water under the boat. I was surprised to see how much there was. I tied my guernsey round my neck and shipped the oars and rowlocks. Then I stood up and stepped out on to the damp stone. "Where's she going to go?" I said.

He jerked his head backwards. "Up there," he said. "A shed. I can lock it. Does she weigh much?"

A cold nose pushed itself suddenly into my hand and I ruffled the silky earflaps. "Hullo, Jack," I said. "No, not much. She's cedar. If you'll pull the bow up, I'll pick up the stern. You could carry her single-handed on the flat."

We lifted the dripping boat out of the water and eased her up. There was a building with double doors, probably in fact a boat-house, standing back a few yards from the top of the steps. We put the pram down inside. He shut and padlocked the doors and dropped the key in his pocket. He said, "Miss Helen said I was to put you in the house. I'll show you. You be all right?"

"I'll be fine. Any chance of something to eat?" I thought, *Miss Helen*. None of your imaginary widowhood for him. Nor apparently of the actual marriage to Cyril Tomlinson. He was an inside man, all right.

He said, "I put something in the kitchen. She said you'd need it."

We went round to the back of the house and he unlocked a door. There was a stone-flagged passage with a door on the right opening into the kitchen. The place felt a bit damp and chilly, but smelt fresh for an empty house. I thought he must keep it well aired. We turned on no lights. There was moonlight in all the windows, and I had my torch. There was a basket on the kitchen table with parcels in it and the neck of a bottle sticking out at one end. On the scrubbed draining board at one side of the sink there was a folded towel and a cake of soap still in its wrapper. The moon shone right on to them. "There's water in this tap," he said, "and in the lavatory across the passage. It's off everywhere else. That be all right?"

"That will be fine. Where do I sleep?"

"Upstairs. I'll show you."

We went along the passage and out into the hall. It was dark here, and he shone his torch ahead of me. We tiptoed up the bare treads of the stairs. At the top he opened a door on the landing. "In here," he said.

The room was at the front of the house. The uncurtained windows looked straight out over the huge sheet of moonlit water. The floor was bare boards, slightly uneven, but polished and very solid. There was a big bed with folded blankets stacked on the mattress and a couple of pillows. Other furniture stood round the walls, but it would all be empty. I went to the window and looked out. Jack was sniffing round the room, his claws tapping on the bare floor, making sure everything was all right. Fenton stood in the doorway. I turned round and said, "It's a nice room. It must have been a lovely house."

He said, "Miss Helen's room, this was." His tone was completely neutral. I nodded, and for a moment neither of us said anything. Then he said, "I'm going to lock you in. That be all right?"

"You do that," I said. "I can always climb out of a downstairs window in case of fire."

"That's right," he said. "I'll be getting on, then. I'll look in in the morning. You won't be going out, I take it?"

"Not if I can help it. Not till tomorrow night's flood." I thought about this for a moment. "You haven't got anything I could read, have you?" I said. "Tomorrow, I mean."

"I'll see what I can find. Good night, then. Come on, Jack."

I said good night to the pair of them and went back to the window. I stood there looking out. I heard him and Jack pad down the stairs and off along the passage, and presently the back door shut. I could not hear the key turn, but I felt sure it had. There was a silver streak in the middle of the estuary now, where the tide was starting to run away down the deep-water channel. The water had a long way to go, and in an hour or two half the sands would be bare to the moon. As I turned back into the room, I caught the faintest possible whiff of a sweet scent in the shut-in air. This had been Helen's room only two years ago. It was natural that it should still just smell of her. I went across to a chest of drawers and pulled one of the top drawers out. It was empty, but the scent was stronger in the drawer than in the room as a whole. I shut the drawer and went down the dark stairs to the moonlit kitchen at the back. Whatever his regrets, a man must eat.

In fact, I ate very well, though at that time of night it must all have come out of Fenton's own larder. There was half a loaf and a lump of butter, still in its wrapper, cut off as it was from a half-pound slab. There was sliced ham, out of a tin but still ham, a good hunk of indeterminate cheese and a few home-pickled onions in the bottom of a teacup with cellophane over the top. Lastly there was a pint bottle of pale ale, an opener and a glass. I had had supper of a sort before I climbed the cliff for the last time, but that was five or six hours ago, and I had done a lot since. I kept the ham for breakfast, but I ate the cheese and onions with about half the bread and butter and all the beer. I felt much better but very sleepy. I stripped down to my vest and pants, unwrapped the cake of soap and washed myself at the moonlit sink. I had forgotten a toothbrush, but I rinsed my mouth as best I could with soap and water. I was not going to sleep dirty in Helen's bed, even if I had to lie alone when I got there.

I left my clothes lying on the kitchen table and tiptoed up the dark stairs on stockinged feet. The scent in the room was clearer now because I was expecting it. I took a last look out of the window.

I still could not see any sand, but the water had a streaky, turbulent look, as if it was moving fast over a shallow bottom. I shivered slightly. I was cold, anyway, and the river frightened me a little. It seemed neither one thing nor the other. But the house felt warm now, especially upstairs, and when I went back to the bed and put a hand on the blankets, I found them soft and bone dry.

There was only one thing I really wanted now. I spread a couple of blankets under me and the rest over. For a minute or two I lay savouring the warmth and comfort, staring up at the reflected moonlight on the ceiling and touched with the insecure, rueful sweetness of lying in Helen's bed. Then I slept.

CHAPTER 17

I WOKE looking up at a white ceiling six feet above my face instead of the varnished wood just over it that I had got used to. When I sat up, the room seemed very spacious and stable in the early-morning light. I thought it was time I had a room of my own like this. Perhaps Helen would be ready to share it with me, seeing that this was hers and she was letting me use it. It was still not six, for all the daylight in the uncurtained windows. I lay down again and rolled over on my side, turning my back to the light. There was still sleep to be had if I gave it a chance, and it might be some time before I got any more. I had all day in front of me and nothing to do until Helen came in the evening. I was happy in a placid, drowsy sort of way. Looking back, I think the day I spent at Herons was the only time during the whole affair when I was consciously and fairly completely happy. It was a miscalculation, of course, but it was a good day at the time. I went to sleep again, savouring my happiness, and when I woke it was past eight.

I got up and went over to the window. It was a clear day, with the leaves of the trees just rustling in the breeze that still came from behind the house. We were sheltered here, admittedly, but then so was *Madge* in her cove under the lee of Bonnet. There was no need to worry about her. The whole expanse of sand was bare in the sunlight. In fact the tide would have turned again and be on its way back up the river, but it would still be some time before it started on its sweep across the flats. The sand looked dry and as firm as tarmac. I thought most of it probably was firm enough, in fact, at this state of the tide. It was when the tide was starting to come over the flats that it might be dangerous anywhere. The sand would liquefy underneath before the water came over the top. The surface that had been firm enough for five or six hours past would still look the same, but it would be as treacherous as the green skin on top of a quagmire. Whether you could actually go right under in it I did not know, but, as Cyril had said, that did not matter. It would hold you until the tide came for you. Whatever the details, the result would be the same. It was a nasty, land-bound sort of way to die, even if it was ultimately salt water you drowned in. Give me deep water and exhaustion every time. That was said to be a peaceful experience, though I had never been clear whose evidence this rested on.

I shivered again, as I had shivered the night before, and from the same mixture of cold and apprehension. I came away from the window, draped myself in a blanket and went downstairs to the kitchen. My clothes were still piled on the end of the table, but Fenton had been up before me. There was a vacuum flask on the corner nearest the door with a clean cup and a small bag of sugar beside it. There were also two paper-backs and a folded newspaper. I turned the books face up. There was a Peter Cheyney, which I had read, and a Cyril Tomlinson, which I had not. It was called *The Seventy-Four*. The cover had a highly coloured picture of warm work on the gun deck. The paper was a copy of the *Tanchester Chronicle* of the day before. I folded it up again as soon as I saw what it was. I poured myself out a cup of Fenton's strong milky tea, pulled a chair into the patch of sunlight by the sink and settled down to drink. I was still draped in my blanket. I felt at peace with the world.

When I had drunk all the tea and got Lemmy Caution

started on his case, I took the blanket off, washed and put my clothes on. I could not shave until I got back to the boat. I hoped Helen would not mind. I told myself firmly that she would do no more than see me by moonlight, and therefore would not. My mind of course ran ahead of my sense of probability and worried about her finding me scrubby to the touch. I even considered borrowing a razor from Fenton, but I thought this would be unlucky. I tidied up myself and the kitchen as best I could. Then I went upstairs, folded the blankets and stacked them on the bed. I was going downstairs to give myself a ham breakfast when I heard the key turn in the back door, and I met Fenton in the kitchen.

"Good morning," I said. "Where's Jack?"

"I left him up at the cottage," he said. "It's better when I'm down here. We'd hear him bark if anything came."

I nodded. I wanted to ask him when he expected Helen, but I did not. I think as much as anything I baulked at calling her Mrs. Tomlinson, but did not think I ought to call her Miss Helen, even to him, much as I like hearing him say it. He said, "You been all right?"

"I've been fine," I said. "You've made me very comfortable." I thought for a moment. "There's one thing," I said. "It'll be high water again about two. I want to watch it come up by daylight. Then when it comes to the night flood, I'll know exactly where we are. That be all right, do you think?"

"I reckon so. So long as you go careful. I'll be up at the cottage keeping an eye on the road."

"How shall I get out, then? Use one of the windows?"

"That'd be better. They can't be seen except from the river. They open easy. But put the catch on again when you come in."

"I'll do that."

He put another small parcel down on the table. "Cheese," he said. "That do you for the day? I can't go out to the shop. I expect Miss Helen will bring something when she comes."

"Fine," I said again. "I've still got the ham. I was going to have that now."

He had gone over to the sink and was staring out of the window. He spoke without turning round. He said, "I take it Miss Helen will be going with you?"

I felt a desperate need to reassure him. "That's what she wants," I said. "It should be all right. I've got the life-jacket for her. There's no wind to speak of, and it will be quiet water all the way."

"That's to your boat?" he said.

"That's right."

He nodded. Then he took a breath and said, "She be coming back?" He turned and looked at me. He had a very direct eye, but his face was quite expressionless.

"I'm afraid that's up to her," I said. "I'm under her orders, same as you are."

He nodded again. "I reckon that's right," he said. "So long as she's safe."

"She'll be as safe as I can make her. I can't say more."

I thought, Damn you, you've got Jack, which is more than I've got. It was too ridiculous to say, but I thought it. I said the next thing that came into my head. I said, "Has Jack sired any pups?"

He looked easier at that, as if we were back on safer ground. "There's a litter due," he said. "About three weeks' time. There's a bitch a couple of miles up the road, at the lodge. It's a good bitch."

"Have you got the pick?"

"I could have. I wasn't going to. One's enough for me."

"Would you like to take a dog for me? I'll come and collect him. When I can."

He said, "I'll do that. Be glad to. All right, I'll be getting back, then." He let himself out and locked the door behind him. I watched him go off across the yard until he disappeared between the buildings. I thought, there's another of us. But I liked him better than I had. I turned back to the table and got down to the ham.

When I had finished it and tidied up, I went back to Lemmy Caution, but found he could not keep my mind fixed. I knew him too well and the house was too quiet. I put the book, open and face down, on the table and went to explore. I thought for a man living alone Charles Casson had made himself comfortable. You could see that, even now. There was nothing cheap or in poor taste anywhere. It was not collector's stuff, but it was old, good and perfectly kept. I had wondered before, when I realised that she owned it, why Helen had left it as it was and what she was thinking of doing with it. Now I wondered more than ever. I supposed, even if she never came back, Cyril could handle it for her. There would be no difficulty over things like that. He would remain anxious to please her, as he was everybody, even if in her case it meant letting her go.

I even wondered whether I might make an offer for the house myself, but it was no good. If it had been almost anywhere else I might have, but not where it stood. I did not like the river. There had been a mystery about Charles Casson, obviously, for him to come and live alone in a place like this. I saw him and Helen's father as one-time partners in doubtful enterprises, living retired and respectable, until his past had caught up with the one and the river with the other. You could not expect Helen to be anything but the person she was. I still thought that, being the people we both were, we might make a fairly successful partnership in our turn. But that was for her to decide.

I went back to the kitchen again, but still could not bring myself to submit to the practised charms of Lemmy Caution. And I did not want to read Cyril's book, not yet. I would read it presently. I had all the day before me. With no particular purpose in mind, but just because it was there, I opened the *Tanchester Chronicle*. I saw it straight away. VISITOR FOUND DROWNED IN LEREMOUTH HARBOUR. I read it all carefully. There was nothing in it, not a shade of meaning anywhere, to suggest anything but accidental death. They had got clean away with it. So far, I thought, so far. It was the last sentence that brought me up short. It said, "*It is believed she had come to Leremouth to meet friends.*" Just that. I put the paper down and sat back, staring out of the window into the sunlit yard.

I wondered who had put that in the reporter's head. I wondered if it was the police, and if so, who had put it in theirs. Or rather, how it had been put there. I knew by whom. I had thought they would keep it in reserve, in case I looked like making trouble. Instead, they had anticipated trouble and were perhaps warning me off. They had me very carefully placed. What I most needed to know was whether they had found *Madge*. They seemed to operate only on land, and she would not be seen from the land unless someone was looking for her pretty systematically and thoroughly. But they might well search for her like that once they realised that she had not arrived anywhere else. If their intelligence system was what I thought it, this would not take them very long. I wished now that I had not agreed to Helen's demand for a rendezvous at Herons. It seemed to be working admirably, but it had wasted twenty-four hours, and I was not at all sure we had twenty-four hours to waste. To convey Helen safely down to *Madge* and then find them already in possession would be irretrievable disaster. I should have to warn Helen of this possibility before we left Herons. I thought she would decide to go all the same, but I had to warn her.

I folded up the paper and then, almost apologetically, shut the Peter Cheyney. It was up to Cyril now to keep my mind occupied until his wife arrived. If the appointment had been a more conventionally gulity one, there might have been some amusement in this. As it was, I could only hope he was up to the job. To my surprise, he was. I know the disparity between authors and their books is a standard joke. Everyone has heard about the man who wears a bow tie and lives in a mews flat and writes books about the good earth, or the prim spinster who sells sex and mayhem. But I had met very few writers, and the thing had not come my way before. The disparity here was not as obvious as that. I had expected authenticity and good taste from Cyril, and got it. What I had not expected was the vitality and assurance. I could see at once why he sold as he did. If I had not known him, I should have been captivated. As it was, I was startled, almost indignant, but I read on. It was as if the man lived so intensely on paper that he had little or nothing left for life elsewhere. Now I came to think of it, it explained so much. I wondered if Helen ever read his books and, if so, what she made of them. I had seen Cyril as the lonely man falling for the appealing widow in the empty house and Helen as consenting, rather against her better judgment, to comfort him in his loneliness. Nothing could be further from the truth. I did not believe Cyril, left to himself, was ever lonely. It would be company he could not stand, the compelling and inevitable company of the sole and constant companion. It was not Helen's better judgment that had been set aside, it was Cyril's. Her judgment had been clear enough.

At half past one I tore myself away from lively doings in the Caribbean and went off into one of the front ground-floor rooms. The tide was well over the flats. It came up on a huge curved front, the centre pushing ahead over the deep-water channel and the wings lapping the banks fifty yards behind the centre. It was still some way from the steps. I pushed the window-catch over and eased up the bottom sash. As Fenton had promised, it moved very easily. I raised it about a foot and then stooped and put my head out. The breeze had gone almost completely, and it was very quiet. I did not think there could be anyone about. I raised the sash a bit further and climbed out. I shut the window behind me, leaving enough of an opening at the bottom for me to get my fingers under. Then I walked down the flagged path to the top of the wall. I suppose if I had thought about it, I should have seen that this was where the danger might be. I myself had first come to Herons walking along the edge of the sand under the wall at very much this state of the tide. If you wanted to approach it unseen, this was the obvious way to come. Luckily, no one had. There was no one waiting under the wall and no one visible along the bank on either side. I went down the steps and considered depths.

I should see presently how far the water actually came. With a tide of this size, there would be far more than was needed to float the pram. I thought the thing to do would be to put the pram on the water as soon as there was a safe depth under it and get out at once into the middle of the river. Even if the tide was still not at full high, the water would be slack, and we could put ourselves where the stream would take hold of us the moment it started to run. I did not know quite what the pram would draw with the two of us in it, but it would not be much even so. I reckoned that when the bottom three steps were covered, we could get afloat. I went back up the steps and found a big whitish stone. I put it on the third step from the bottom, close against the wall. Then I went up the steps again and leant over the wall and looked at it. You could see it well enough, even in the moonlight. All we had to do was wait until the stone was awash, and then move. I waited now and watched the water come.

The stone was awash by ten to two. According to the book, it should be awash again at a quarter past two in the morning. That was it, then. I watched the water cover another two steps and then went back into the house. There was no point in hanging about where I might be seen. It did not matter how high the tide came up the steps, either now or in the morning. I had got all I needed. Also, I wanted to get back to the Caribbean.

I saw the seventy-four safe back into Portsmouth long before it even started to get dark. After that there was nothing to do but wait for it to get dark and wonder how soon, once it did, Helen would come. For the first time since the start of that unreal, isolated day I felt an undeniable crawl of apprehension.

But the apprehension was overlaid with longing. I wanted Helen here. I wanted her to myself in this quiet house for as long as possible before the water came up to the white stone outside and we had to go out and commit ourselves to the river and moonlight. That was the part I was apprehensive about, but there must be something I could look forward to before that.

It got dark early in the house with the trees standing over it. After a bit I went upstairs. I spread a blanket over the bed and put the rest on a chair. Then I took my shoes off and lay down with my head on the pillow, staring up at the ceiling and listening to the silence. I do not know what time it was when I went to sleep or when I woke up. I only know that when I woke up it was quite dark and there was someone coming upstairs. I sat up and swung my legs off the bed. The door opened and Helen came in. She smelt the same as the room did, bringing back to it what it had been slowly losing these two years. She shut the door behind her and came and sat beside me on the bed.

"Well?" she said.

CHAPTER 18

IT WAS a clear night outside, but the moon was not yet up. I peered at Helen in the glimmer from the windows, trying to make out what her mood was and where I stood with her. I had to try afresh, every time we met. There was no carry-over from one meeting to the next. I wondered what would happen if we were continuously together for any length of time. I supposed I was due, at this very moment, to start finding out. Meanwhile I peered at her in the gloom. She was smiling slightly. She seemed very friendly and matter-of-fact. I said, "All well here, I think."

"When can we leave?"

"A quarter past two. That's the earliest. If we left any time in the following hour, it would probably be all right." I looked at my watch. It was about ten to eleven.

She said, "We'll go at a quarter past two."

"What about you?"

She was still smiling slightly. "What about me?" she said.

"I mean—about your end. Are you clear, do you think?"

"I can't tell. I hope so. I just drove straight down. Fenton let me in from the road and I came straight down to the house."

"Your car's here?"

"In the yard, yes. There was nothing else I could do."

"I suppose not. Where's Fenton?"

"He's up at the cottage. He's coming down at eleven to get a time. Then he'll go back to the cottage and watch the road."

I thought. "Better tell him to come at two," I said. "There's no point in his coming earlier. Once the water's there, it won't take us five minutes to put the boat down and get off."

She said, "All right. I'll tell him to stay on the gate till two. I've got a bag, by the way. A zipper bag, quite small. Is that all right?"

"Of course. You've got to have something. I should have told you. Have you got what you wanted from here?"

"Not yet. I'll get it. I'd better go down and tell Fenton first. I've got some food, by the way. Would you like some? You can't have had much today."

"Before we go, certainly. I'm afraid it will be all tins on board."

She got up and went to the door. It struck me that she went downstairs much less quietly than I did. She was not noisy about it, but I tiptoed everywhere in that house and, when I talked, talked in whispers. She took it all in her stride. I suppose that was natural enough. She simply felt at home. I got up and put my shoes on. Then I stood by the window, waiting for her to come back.

She came after about five minutes. She did not come right into the room. She put her head round the door and said, "There's food in the kitchen. We'd better have it now, I think." I followed her downstairs. You could, I suppose, call it picnic food, but it was pretty rarefied, and there was a bottle of wine to go with it. There was very little light in the kitchen, less even than upstairs, but by this time our eyes were used to it. We talked hardly at all. I found I was very hungry. We ate all there was between us. I ate very much more than half the food, but I think we split the bottle evenly. My apprehension was gone. So was my placidity. I was full of an enormous and rather breathless exhilaration.

When we had finished, she put the things together at one end of the table. "Fenton will look after those," she said. She went out into the hall and up the stairs, and I followed her. She said, "I'd better get that key." She went back into her own room, which had been my room for the past twenty-odd hours. "Do you want to see?" she said. "it's childish really, but quite ingenious." She walked across the room and flashed a torch on the panelling behind the dressing table. She moved something, and a little cupboard opened in the wall. She took out something that glinted in the torchlight. It was a key on a fine steel chain. It looked a fairly elaborate key, but I only got a glimpse of it. She put the chain over her neck and dropped the key inside her clothes. She flashed the light on the cupboard in the panelling again. "Charles Casson discovered it when he was doing the house," she said. "Someone's cache, I suppose, once. He showed me when I came. No one else knew about it. I left the key there when I married Cyril. It seemed as good a place as any."

"The key's what you'll need over there?"

"That's right. There's a safe of sorts. Of course they'd get it open if they found it. They'd use explosives or something. But I don't see why I should." She slid the panel back and the cupboard disappeared.

"This was your room?" I said.

"Yes."

"Do you mind my using it?"

"No. I told Fenton."

"It smells of you still."

"Does it?"

She went over and sat on the bed, and I stood looking down at her. I had my back to what light there was, but I could see her face quite clearly looking up at me. I said, "Why have you left the place like this? Didn't you want to get rid of it?"

"I couldn't, don't you see? It's not mine, not at law. Charles Casson didn't make a will. He didn't expect to die like that. And of course I'm not his natural heir. Everyone assumes it's mine, and I think he wanted me to have it. But I can't sell it without proving my title, and of course I haven't got one. I couldn't even start without letting it come out who I was."

"Of course. I hadn't thought of that. Does Cyril know?"

She shook her head. "Fenton," she said. "Not Cyril."

I said, "Poor Cyril."

"Why poor Cyril? He's all right."

"He will be now, I think."

"You mean, now I've gone?"

"I think so, yes."

She said, "Come here where I can see you." I sat down on the bed beside her, and she looked at me for a moment. She said, "You're not simple, at all, are you?"

"I don't think so, of course. I don't suppose anybody thinks himself simple. Do you think Cyril is?"

"Fairly simple, yes."

"Have you read any of his books?"

"No. I didn't think he wanted me to."

"You're very likely right about that. You ought to, all the same."

"Have you?"

"I read one today for the first time."

"And you don't think he's even fairly simple?"

"Not now, no. I did, I admit."

She nodded. She seemed cheerful and interested, as if we were talking about someone we had both just met. "What's the time?" she said.

I looked at my watch. "Getting on for twelve."

"Two hours to wait," she said. She kicked off her shoes and swung her feet up on to the bed. She separated the two pillows and put them side by side. Then she moved over and lay with her head on the farther one, but her head was turned sideways, looking at me.

I leant over and took my shoes off. "May I join you?" I said.

"Yes."

I lay down beside her on the bed, but not on my back. I leant sideways on one elbow, looking down at her. I said, "Do you think you could find use for my non-simplicity?"

"You put it very disarmingly."

"I think you would take a great deal of disarming. Has anyone ever disarmed you? Except yourself, of course."

She said, "You ask too many questions." She turned suddenly and reached out her arms to me. "Come here," she said, "and stop talking for a bit."

It could hardly have been more different from the first time we had made love. Then there had been total surrender on her part and as a person I might hardly have existed. Now it was all very quiet and friendly, and when I looked at her face, right up to the last, it was smiling. At the last, of course, the smile went and the blank, idiot-face stared up at nothing, but then the face turned back to me and the smile came back, first into her eyes and then on to her lips. "You make love very nicely," she said. "Now let's try to sleep for a little. Then we must go."

We lay on our sides, face to face, but with only our hands touching. She went to sleep almost at once. I did not. I must have slept for a couple of hours before she came, and I did not need the sleep. I lay watching her for what seemed quite a long time. It cannot really have been very long. She slept very quietly and peacefully, as if she had not a care in the world. I told myself she must trust me to sleep like that, and that gave me in my turn a feeling of ease and security. I slept myself in the end, but I think not for very long. When I woke, the moon was up and the whole world outside the windows flooded with light. My watch said nearly half past one. I got very gently off the bed and went to the window. You could see the whole stretch of the sands, almost more clearly than by daylight, because there was no dazzle. The water was not yet in sight, but it would not be very far away.

I took my guernsey off and put on the life-jacket I had dropped in one corner of the room. The plastic made a stealthy rustling sound, and I heard Helen move on the bed. She said,

"What are you doing?"

"Putting on my life-jacket. There's one for you. Better wear it underneath a jersey or something. It's downstairs."

She sat up and stared at the moonlight outside the windows. She said, "What time is it?"

"About half past one." I went over and knelt at the side of the bed. I said, "Helen—" but she swung her legs off the far side of the bed away from me.

She said, "I must get my bag. It's in the car."

I got up. "All right," I said. "Have you got a key?"

"Of the house? Of course. Haven't you?"

"Fenton's got it.

She made a small amused noise. "Fenton,"she said. She went to the door.

I said, "Shall I come?"

"No, I won't be a minute."

She shut the door behind her and went down the stairs. I pulled on my guernsey over my life-jacket and put my shoes on. Then I went back to the window and waited. The night was almost completely still. The shadow of the trees which lay across the house had no movement in it at all. The sky I could see was all cloudless. The moonlight was almost too bright, brighter than we needed. I thought of drifting down past the harbour mouth, and wondered if there would be room for both of us to get down behind the gunwales of the boat. Perhaps it would not matter so much if anyone did see us when we were going down.

I began to wonder what had happened to Helen. She had only to get her bag from the car, and the car was standing in the yard, just outside the back door. My assurance drained out of me, and I felt a sudden apprehension that something had gone wrong. I started to go towards the door, but stopped. Helen had told me to wait here. Better do what she said. Something had simply held her up. There was nothing to show that anything was wrong, except the crawling in my stomach. I made a move towards the door again, but again hesitated. It was the hesitation that saved me. I heard the kitchen door open and footsteps in the hall at the bottom of the stairs. There was something odd about them. I stayed where I was, close to the door. They started up the stairs, and I knew that there were two of them, two pairs of feet coming up the stairs, one behind the other. Just before they got to the top they stopped.

A man's voice said, "Go on." He spoke quite softly. It was not Fenton's voice.

Then I heard Helen's voice, very loud and clear on the opposite side of the door. She said, "Why should I? Why should I make it easy for you?" The tone was plaintive, almost whining. I could not reconcile it at all with any picture I had of Helen. It was completely false and unfamiliar. Then I knew what I had to do. I tiptoed across the floor and stood flat against the wall, where the door would open across me. The footsteps came on again, and someone started to open the door. I could not see her, because the door hid her as she opened it. She opened it slowly and swung it right back until it actually touched me as I stood against the wall behind it. I thought she gave it a little extra push then, as if to make sure that I was on the other side of it. She said, "The key's over there in a cupboard."

The man said, "Get it, then."

I heard her start across the room and the man's footsteps following her. Then she stopped and said, "Did you have to kill that girl?"

I began to move the door back a fraction of an inch at a time. The man said, "What girl?"

I moved the door a little more and got one eye round it. Helen was standing over near the dressing table. She was facing towards me but not looking at me at all. She was looking at the man who stood between us. He stood facing her with his back to me. His hands hung loose at this sides. They looked more menacing than any weapon. In any case, he did not want to kill her. He had to have her alive. It was not my Mr. Matthews. She said, "The girl in the harbour."

I came round the edge of the door and began to go forward, measuring the distance all the time with my eyes fixed on the back of the man's neck. Just for a fraction of a second she let her eyes meet mine. Then she turned and began groping rather clumsily over the panelling. Her hands made just enough noise on the wood to take the edge off the silence. The man said, "She was trying to talk to your big friend."

Helen said, "Mr. Curtis? But he's gone?"

The man said, "That's what it looks like. But he'd served his purpose." I was quite close to him now. I was going to kill him. I was not quite clear what this would involve, but I had no doubt at all of the end product. I turned my right side to him, and brought my hand up over my left shoulder. At the same moment Helen stopped what she was doing and swung round. Her face was like a mask, with the eyes wide and blank. He heard me behind him, of course, but he did the wrong thing. It takes a very highly trained man not to. He swung round instead of ducking forwards, and the edge of my hand caught the side of his neck as he turned. He went down on his knees with his head over sideways. I do not think he was dead. I have never dared to make myself adept at that sort of thing. I took him by the neck and lifted him till his feet were off the floor. It was what he had done to Celia, only he had held her under the water and I held him up in the air. There was complete silence except for the noise his legs made. After a bit even that stopped. Then there was only my rather noisy breathing. Helen had not moved.

I let him down on the floor and rolled him on his back. I felt his heart, but there was nothing there. He did not seem to have any sort of weapon on him. Helen was still standing there, looking down at the pair of us. I said, "What happened? Where was he?" I whispered, and now even she whispered in reply.

"Outside the back door. He was waiting. There's no car. They must have come along the river. Or across the fields. Otherwise Fenton would have seen them."

"They? Did you see the other one?"

"No, but he'll be somewhere. At the front of the house, I expect."

I got up and looked at my watch. I said, "Fenton will be coming down in a quarter of an hour. I'll have to go and see what I can do. You'd better wait here." I looked at the man on the floor. There was no direct moonlight in the room, but you could see things pretty clearly. "Do you mind?" I said.

"I don't mind. Only be careful."

"I will." I tiptoed down the dark stairs and along the passage. The door into the kitchen was open. The moonlight streamed into the room. There was no one there. The back door was shut, but the key was on the inside. I turned the handle and began to open the door very slowly.

I supposed it was Mr. Matthews I had to deal with, but I did not know where he was or how much he knew. I did not even know if he had seen Helen come into the house and his brother, if they were brothers, go in with her. The one thing I did know was that he was not expecting me. Once I could locate him, this ought to give me the advantage. But I did not know where to start looking for him, and in this moonlight the chances of my seeing him first seemed very small. The other one had not been armed, but I felt much less sure about Mr. Matthews. Physical violence would not be his line, and I did not think he would leave himself unprotected. I did not like it a bit.

I got the door open wide enough and looked out into the moonlit yard. There was no one there and no obvious place of concealment. The doors of the different buildings were shut. Helens' car stood there with one of its rear doors open. I could even see her zipper bag on the back seat, but there was no one in the car. There was nothing else for it. I opened the door a little wider and went out into the moonlight. For what seemed a very long time I stood there, with my back to the back wall of the house, waiting for something to happen. Nothing did. I turned right-handed and began to make my way round to the front of the house.

If Mr. Matthews was watching the front, it was no good my going through the gate under the arch and round to the door. I had to make a wider circle and if possible come up behind him. I tiptoed across to the shed where we had put the pram. I was in the shadow of the trees again here. I doubt if it made all that difference, but I felt easier. From there I made my way to the river wall. Then I stopped and looked along the front of the house. The dappled shadow of the trees was over everything, but at least it did not move. It was movement I was looking for. I could not see any. The big, unpruned rose-bushes stood about in fantastic shapes. The roses had the rather sickly smell of flowers that are past their best. There were half a dozen places where a man might be standing and where I should never see him unless he moved. I went along the wall inch by inch, never taking my eyes off the breathless, dappled stretch of light and shade in front of the house. I got to the gap in the wall where the steps went down to the sand, and then it happened.

I suppose he had been watching me for some time. Long enough, anyhow, for him to recognise me and come to the conclusion that something had gone wrong. At any rate, he did not stop to ask questions. He fired from where he was. I still do not know where that was. All I know is that the bullet cut a straight gash along the side of my guernsey, with only the thickness of the life-jacket between it and my ribs, and that I went down the steps so fast that I was lucky not to break my ankle. I ran a few steps and found myself in full moonlight. I looked back, saw something move at the top of the steps and started running again. He fired as I moved. The bullet thudded into the sand behind me. I ran another fifty yards before I looked back again. He was coming after me, running as fast as I was. There were just the two of us in that huge stretch of moonlit sand. Sooner or later he would wing me, and that would be that. I turned right-handed and ran straight down towards the advancing tide.

I remembered what Cyril had said about keeping your head and doing the right thing. I hoped he was right. I thought my life-jacket ought to help. Even so, when it happened, it was very frightening. I saw the white creamed edge of the tide slipping over the sand about fifteen yards ahead of me. It did not make a sound. Then the sand I put my foot on simply caved in, and I was up to my knees, held fast and sinking all the time. Mr. Matthews fired again a second before I went down. It was that that settled him. He thought he had hit me and came on to finish me off. I went flat down on my back, almost out of my mind with fright, but still trying to do the right thing. I wrenched one foot out of the sand, and lay there for a moment, trying to collect my wits. The other foot was still stuck. But I knew that my body was not sinking. It had settled down in a puddle of wet sand, and lay there like a stranded log. I rolled over and wrenched at the other leg. The water was all round me now, rippling past me and soaking into my clothes and hair. A moment later my foot came free, and I lay there inert, waiting for the water to lift me clear of the sand.

I lifted my head and looked at Mr. Matthews. He was standing there in the moonlight, not twenty yards away from me. He still had his gun in his hand, but he was not looking at me. He was looking down at the sand round his feet. He knew I was still alive. He had seen me struggling, but probably did not realise until it was too late what had happened to me. Then he lifted his head and looked at me, and for a moment we stared at each other, with me flat on my back in the water and him standing on the sand. He brought the gun up in a very careful aim, and then his legs went from under him. The gun went off, but the bullet may have gone anywhere. He was on his hands and knees now, trying to crawl, but his hands went in as well as his feet. He pulled them out and leant back. His legs were sunk almost to the hips. Then the tide lifted me, and I began to drift very gently up-river past him. I passed within a few yards of him. He did not look at me at all. He was looking at the sand round his waist and the water that frothed gently over it.

I paddled carefully with my hands, edging myself out into the deeper water. The next time I looked back, there was nothing to see but a flat stretch of moving water with the moon shining on it. Then something broke surface. An arm came out and waved aimlessly in the air, as if it was looking for something it could not find. Then it went under again. I turned on my front and began swimming steadily across the stream towards the west bank of the river.

CHAPTER 19

When I got nearer to the bank, the water was very shallow. I swam as flat as I could, with the life-jacket floating me unnaturally high on the surface. Even so, I touched the bottom occasionally, and when I did, I pulled my foot away as if I had touched something alive and menacing under the water. This was ridiculous, of course. With the amount of water there was under me, I could not have got myself caught in the sand now if I had tried. But it had caught me once, and it scared the life out of me. I drifted well up-stream from Herons before I got close to the bank. The next thing I knew, there was a big black face on the water, heading out towards me from the shore and grinning as it came. I called "Jack!" and a moment later he was alongside, steering himself with his massive tail and moving as easily as he moved on land. Most Labradors can outswim a man over any sort of distance. I did not need his help, but I was glad to have him with me. We came ashore together. The sand when I put my foot on it was perfectly firm. Jack shook himself in a cloud of moonlit spray and gambolled round me as I started to walk back along the bank.

Helen and Fenton were standing together in the shade under the trees. Jack ran up to Fenton as pleased with himself as if he had brought in a difficult bird. Helen said, "What happened? I heard shooting."

"He's gone," I said. "In the river." I looked at Fenton. "What will happen?" I said. "He was well down in the sand."

He said, "The tide will have him out of it. He'll come ashore somewhere. Is he marked?"

"Not by me."

He nodded. "Another visitor drowned in the river," he said.

"Two," said Helen. "Only the other one won't be found." She seemed very satisfied with the arrangement.

Fenton said, "Good thing they didn't bring their car here."

I stood there looking from one to the other of them. Then I turned and walked to the top of the steps. My white stone was well under the surface, but there were two wet steps clear of the water. It was falling already. I said to Fenton, "Give me a hand with the pram." He looked at me for a moment without saying anything. Then he nodded.

"I'll get the key," he said. "I came down in a bit of a hurry." He turned and walked off through the yard with Jack beside him.

Helen said, "But there's no need now. They're both dead. I needn't go now."

"No?" I said. "That's up to you. I've got to get back to the boat."

"But you're wet," she said. It seemed an odd point to pick on in a complex situation, but it had its merits.

"I can't help that," I said. "I've got to get the pram back to the boat, and there's no other way of doing it. It's a mild night, God knows, and I'll be rowing. I shan't catch cold."

She nodded but said nothing. We stood there at the top of the steps, waiting for Fenton to come back with the key. It was like waiting for a train to leave. The pressure of time falsified everything. By the time I saw him coming back across the yard there was another step showing above water. I said, "You'll be all right now."

She said, "Yes." She seemed a little uncertain.

"I mean, you can choose your own time. Don't put it off too long."

She looked as if she was going to say something but thought better of it. Finally she said, "No. No, I'll be all right," and I heard Fenton unlocking the shed.

We got the pram down to the water with a step to spare. I wondered how long the white stone would stay where it was. I got myself settled while Fenton held the boat against the steps. He said, "About that pup—"

"Pick a good one," I said. "Go for the broadest head in the litter. I'll be back." We spoke quietly, down there at the bottom of the steps. Helen was looking down at us from the top. I did not think she could hear what we were saying. "Shove her off," I said. I leant back on the oars and a moment later I was out in the full glare of the moon. I rowed half a dozen strokes. Then I easied and waved a hand. I could not see Fenton. I could just see Helen's white face in the dappled shade under the trees. She raised a hand in reply. I took the oars again and headed out for the middle of the river.

Leremouth was drowned in the moonlight as it had been more than twenty-four hours before. There were no lights anywhere except at the harbour mouth. I did not know what was going on there now. I only knew that it was nothing to do with me and that I should never come back to it. I would fetch my pup by road and from the north. I rowed steadily on down-river, not caring who saw me go.

The breeze met me, blowing in from the sea, as I crept under the eastern side of Bonnet. The tide had almost stopped running now, and I had quite a hard row of it at the end. I think I looked over my shoulder half a dozen times and saw nothing. The next time I looked I saw *Madge* sitting there, quite close, and so white in the moon that she looked almost phosphorescent. It never occurred to me that there might be anyone waiting for me. That was all over. Nobody knew where *Madge* was, and it would not matter if they did. In fact no one was. I made the pram fast and clambered aboard, making as much noise as I liked. The cockpit was full of the nylon line I had thrown there before I came away. I coiled it and got it stowed in the fo'c'sle before I changed my clothes.

As soon as I was ready, I got sail up and put the pram out on the end of its towing warp. I set the motor running in neutral and went forward to the anchor. We motored out into a very light southerly blowing steady and straight in from the sea. I cut the motor, sheeted in and headed due east. There was no sound anywhere but the gentle ripple of our way on the water.

When I had closed the mouth of the Lere, I turned and looked back at Bonnet. It lay in a long line of shadow astern, but right on top of it and out near the end a single yellow light showed. I knew what it was. It was the light in Cyril's work-room. The night was nearly over now. The moon was well over in the west and any time now there would be daylight over the land northeastwards, but up on Bonnet Cyril was still in his work-room. I thought perhaps he was waiting for his wife to come home. Then I thought perhaps he was there because she had. I did not know which.

P. M. HUBBARD

P. M. Hubbard was born in 1910 and was educated at Oxford University, where he won the Newdigate Prize for English Verse in 1933. From 1934 to 1947 he served in the Indian Civil Service, and upon its disbandment in 1947 he returned to England to work for the British Council in London. He resigned from that job in 1951 to free-lance as a writer, and contributed verse, features and even Parliamentary reports to *Punch*. Later he entered business as deputy director of an industrial organization, but again resigned to earn his living as a writer. Mr. Hubbard's previous novels are *Flush as May*, *Picture of Millie*, *A Hive of Glass*, *The Holm Oaks*, *The Tower*, *The Country of Again* and *Cold Waters*.

THE PERENNIAL LIBRARY MYSTERY SERIES

E. C. Bentley

TRENT'S LAST CASE
"One of the three best detective stories ever written."
—Agatha Christie

TRENT'S OWN CASE
"I won't waste time saying that the plot is sound and the detection satisfying. Trent has not altered a scrap and reappears with all his old humor and charm." —Dorothy L. Sayers

Gavin Black

A DRAGON FOR CHRISTMAS
"Potent excitement!" —*New York Herald Tribune*

THE EYES AROUND ME
"I stayed up until all hours last night reading *The Eyes Around Me,* which is something I do not do very often, but I was so intrigued by the ingeniousness of Mr. Black's plotting and the witty way in which he spins his mystery. I can only say that I enjoyed the book enormously."
—F. van Wyck Mason

YOU WANT TO DIE, JOHNNY?
"Gavin Black doesn't just develop a pressure plot in suspense, he adds uninfected wit, character, charm, and sharp knowledge of the Far East to make rereading as keen as the first race-through." —*Book Week*

Nicholas Blake

THE BEAST MUST DIE
"It remains one more proof that in the hands of a really first-class writer the detective novel can safely challenge comparison with any other variety of fiction." —*The Manchester Guardian*

THE CORPSE IN THE SNOWMAN
"If there is a distinction between the novel and the detective story (which we do not admit), then this book deserves a high place in both categories." —*The New York Times*

THE DREADFUL HOLLOW
"Pace unhurried, characters excellent, reasoning solid."
—*San Francisco Chronicle*

END OF CHAPTER
". . . admirably solid . . . an adroit formal detective puzzle backed up by firm characterization and a knowing picture of London publishing."
—*The New York Times*

HEAD OF A TRAVELER
"Another grade A detective story of the right old jigsaw persuasion."
—*New York Herald Tribune Book Review*

MINUTE FOR MURDER
"An outstanding mystery novel. Mr. Blake's writing is a delight in itself."
—*The New York Times*

THE MORNING AFTER DEATH
"One of Blake's best."
—Rex Warner

A PENKNIFE IN MY HEART
"Style brilliant . . . and suspenseful."
—*San Francisco Chronicle*

THE PRIVATE WOUND
[Blake's] best novel in a dozen years . . . . An intensely penetrating study of sexual passion . . . . A powerful story of murder and its aftermath."
—Anthony Boucher, *The New York Times*

A QUESTION OF PROOF
"The characters in this story are unusually well drawn, and the suspense is well sustained."
—*The New York Times*

THE SAD VARIETY
"It is a stunner. I read it instead of eating, instead of sleeping."
—Dorothy Salisbury Davis

THERE'S TROUBLE BREWING
"Nigel Strangeways is a puzzling mixture of simplicity and penetration, but all the more real for that."
—*The Times Literary Supplement*

THOU SHELL OF DEATH
"It has all the virtues of culture, intelligence and sensibility that the most exacting connoisseur could ask of detective fiction."
—*The Times* [London] *Literary Supplement*

THE WHISPER IN THE GLOOM
"One of the most entertaining suspense-pursuit novels in many seasons."
—*The New York Times*

THE WIDOW'S CRUISE
"A stirring suspense. . . . The thrilling tale leaves nothing to be desired."
—*Springfield Republican*

THE WORM OF DEATH
"It [The Worm of Death] is one of Blake's very best—and his best is better than almost anyone's." —Louis Untermeyer

John & Emery Bonett

A BANNER FOR PEGASUS
"A gem! Beautifully plotted and set. . . . Not only is the murder adroit and deserved, and the detection competent, but the love story is charming." —Jacques Barzun and Wendell Hertig Taylor

DEAD LION
"A clever plot, authentic background and interesting characters highly recommended this one." —*New Republic*

Christianna Brand

GREEN FOR DANGER
"You have to reach for the greatest of Great Names (Christie, Carr, Queen . . .) to find Brand's rivals in the devious subtleties of the trade."
—Anthony Boucher

TOUR DE FORCE
"Complete with traps for the over-ingenious, a double-reverse surprise ending and a key clue planted so fairly and obviously that you completely overlook it. If that's your idea of perfect entertainment, then seize at once upon *Tour de Force.*" —Anthony Boucher, *The New York Times*

Marjorie Carleton

VANISHED
"Exceptional . . . a minor triumph."
—Jacques Barzun and Wendell Hertig Taylor, *A Catalogue of Crime*

George Harmon Coxe

MURDER WITH PICTURES
"[Coxe] has hit the bull's-eye with his first shot."
—*The New York Times*

Edmund Crispin

BURIED FOR PLEASURE
"Absolute and unalloyed delight."
—Anthony Boucher, *The New York Times*

D. M. Devine

MY BROTHER'S KILLER
"A most enjoyable crime story which I enjoyed reading down to the last moment."
—Agatha Christie

Kenneth Fearing

THE BIG CLOCK
"It will be some time before chill-hungry clients meet again so rare a compound of irony, satire, and icy-fingered narrative. *The Big Clock* is . . . a psychothriller you won't put down." —*Weekly Book Review*

Andrew Garve

THE ASHES OF LODA
"Garve . . . embellishes a fine fast adventure story with a more credible picture of the U.S.S.R. than is offered in most thrillers."
—*The New York Times Book Review*

THE CUCKOO LINE AFFAIR
". . . an agreeable and ingenious piece of work." —*The New Yorker*

A HERO FOR LEANDA
"One can trust Mr. Garve to put a fresh twist to any situation, and the ending is really a lovely surprise." —*The Manchester Guardian*

MURDER THROUGH THE LOOKING GLASS
". . . refreshingly out-of-the-way and enjoyable . . . highly recommended to all comers." —*Saturday Review*

NO TEARS FOR HILDA
"It starts fine and finishes finer. I got behind on breathing watching Max get not only his man but his woman, too." —Rex Stout

THE RIDDLE OF SAMSON
"The story is an excellent one, the people are quite likable, and the writing is superior." —*Springfield Republican*

Michael Gilbert

BLOOD AND JUDGMENT
"Gilbert readers need scarcely be told that the characters all come alive at first sight, and that his surpassing talent for narration enhances any plot. . . . Don't miss." —*San Francisco Chronicle*

THE BODY OF A GIRL
"Does what a good mystery should do: open up into all kinds of ramifications, with untold menace behind the action. At the end, there is a bang-up climax, and it is a pleasure to see how skilfully Gilbert wraps everything up." —*The New York Times Book Review*

THE DANGER WITHIN
"Michael Gilbert has nicely combined some elements of the straight detective story with plenty of action, suspense, and adventure, to produce a superior thriller." —*Saturday Review*

DEATH HAS DEEP ROOTS
"Trial scenes superb; prowl along Loire vivid chase stuff; funny in right places; a fine performance throughout." —*Saturday Review*

FEAR TO TREAD
"Merits serious consideration as a work of art."
—*The New York Times*

C. W. Grafton

BEYOND A REASONABLE DOUBT
"A very ingenious tale of murder . . . a brilliant and gripping narrative."
—Jacques Barzun and Wendell Hertig Taylor

Edward Grierson

THE SECOND MAN
"One of the best trial-testimony books to have come along in quite a while." —*The New Yorker*

Cyril Hare

DEATH IS NO SPORTSMAN
"You will be thrilled because it succeeds in placing an ingenious story in a new and refreshing setting. . . . The identity of the murderer is really a surprise." —*Daily Mirror*

DEATH WALKS THE WOODS
"Here is a fine formal detective story, with a technically brilliant solution demanding the attention of all connoisseurs of construction."
—Anthony Boucher, *The New York Times Book Review*

AN ENGLISH MURDER
"By a long shot, the best crime story I have read for a long time. Everything is traditional, but originality does not suffer. The setting is perfect. Full marks to Mr. Hare." —*Irish Press*

TRAGEDY AT LAW
"An extremely urbane and well-written detective story."
—*The New York Times*

UNTIMELY DEATH
"The English detective story at its quiet best, meticulously underplayed, rich in perceivings of the droll human animal and ready at the last with a neat surprise which has been there all the while had we but wits to see it." —*New York Herald Tribune Book Review*

WITH A BARE BODKIN
"One of the best detective stories published for a long time."
—*The Spectator*

Robert Harling

THE ENORMOUS SHADOW
"In some ways the best spy story of the modern period. . . . The writing is terse and vivid . . . the ending full of action . . . altogether first-rate."
—Jacques Barzun and Wendell Hertig Taylor, *A Catalogue of Crime*

Matthew Head

THE CABINDA AFFAIR
"An absorbing whodunit and a distinguished novel of atmosphere."
—Anthony Boucher, *The New York Times*

MURDER AT THE FLEA CLUB
"The true delight is in Head's style, its limpid ease combined with humor and an awesome precision of phrase." —*San Francisco Chronicle*

M. V. Heberden

ENGAGED TO MURDER
"Smooth plotting." —*The New York Times*

James Hilton

WAS IT MURDER?
"The story is well planned and well written."
—*The New York Times*

P. M. Hubbard

HIGH TIDE
"A smooth elaboration of mounting horror and danger."
—*Library Journal*

Elspeth Huxley

THE AFRICAN POISON MURDERS
"Obscure venom, manical mutilations, deadly bush fire, thrilling climax compose major opus.... Top-flight."
—*Saturday Review of Literature*

Francis Iles

BEFORE THE FACT
"Not many 'serious' novelists have produced character studies to compare with Iles's internally terrifying portrait of the murderer in *Before the Fact,* his masterpiece and a work truly deserving the appellation of unique and beyond price." —Howard Haycraft

MALICE AFORETHOUGHT
"It is a long time since I have read anything so good as *Malice Aforethought,* with its cynical humour, acute criminology, plausible detail and rapid movement. It makes you hug yourself with pleasure."
—H. C. Harwood, *Saturday Review*

Michael Innes

DEATH BY WATER *(available 4/82)*
"The amount of ironic social criticism and deft characterization of scenes and people would serve another author for six books."
—Jacques Barzun and Wendell Hertig Taylor

Michael Innes (cont'd)

THE LONG FAREWELL *(available 4/82)*
"A model of the deft, classic detective story, told in the most wittily diverting prose." —*The New York Times*

Mary Kelly

THE SPOILT KILL
"Mary Kelly is a new Dorothy Sayers. . . . [An] exciting new novel." —*Evening News*

Lange Lewis

THE BIRTHDAY MURDER
"Almost perfect in its playlike purity and delightful prose." —Jacques Barzun and Wendell Hertig Taylor

Arthur Maling

LUCKY DEVIL
"The plot unravels at a fast clip, the writing is breezy and Maling's approach is as fresh as today's stockmarket quotes." —*Louisville Courier Journal*

RIPOFF
"A swiftly paced story of today's big business is larded with intrigue as a Ralph Nader-type investigates an insurance scandal and is soon on the run from a hired gun and his brother. . . . Engrossing and credible." —*Booklist*

SCHROEDER'S GAME
"As the title indicates, this Schroeder is up to something, and the unravelling of his game is a diverting and sufficiently blood-soaked entertainment." —*The New Yorker*

Thomas Sterling

THE EVIL OF THE DAY
"Prose as witty and subtle as it is sharp and clear. . .characters unconventionally conceived and richly bodied forth . . . . In short, a novel to be treasured." —Anthony Boucher, *The New York Times*

Julian Symons

THE BELTING INHERITANCE
"A superb whodunit in the best tradition of the detective story."
—August Derleth, *Madison Capital Times*

BLAND BEGINNING
"Mr. Symons displays a deft storytelling skill, a quiet and literate wit, a nice feeling for character, and detectival ingenuity of a high order."
—Anthony Boucher, *The New York Times*

BOGUE'S FORTUNE
"There's a touch of the old sardonic humour, and more than a touch of style."
—*The Spectator*

THE BROKEN PENNY
"The most exciting, astonishing and believable spy story to appear in years.
—Anthony Boucher, *The New York Times Book Review*

THE COLOR OF MURDER
"A singularly unostentatious and memorably brilliant detective story."
—*New York Herald Tribune Book Review*

THE 31ST OF FEBRUARY
"Nobody has painted a more gruesome picture of the advertising business since Dorothy Sayers wrote 'Murder Must Advertise', and very few people have written a more entertaining or dramatic mystery story."
—*The New Yorker*

Dorothy Stockbridge Tillet
(John Stephen Strange)

THE MAN WHO KILLED FORTESCUE
"Better than average."
—*Saturday Review of Literature*

Simon Troy

SWIFT TO ITS CLOSE
"A nicely literate British mystery . . . the atmosphere and the plot are exceptionally well wrought, the dialogue excellent."
—*Best Sellers*

Henry Wade

A DYING FALL
"One of those expert British suspense jobs . . . it crackles with undercurrents of blackmail, violent passion and murder. Topnotch in its class."
—*Time*

THE HANGING CAPTAIN
"This is a detective story for connoisseurs, for those who value clear thinking and good writing above mere ingenuity and easy thrills."
—*Times Literary Supplement*

Hillary Waugh

LAST SEEN WEARING . . .
"A brilliant tour de force." —Julian Symons

THE MISSING MAN
"The quiet detailed police work of Chief Fred C. Fellows, Stockford, Conn., is at its best in *The Missing Man* . . . one of the Chief's toughest cases and one of the best handled."
—Anthony Boucher, *The New York Times Book Review*

Henry Kitchell Webster

WHO IS THE NEXT?
"A double murder, private-plane piloting, a neat impersonation, and a delicate courtship are adroitly combined by a writer who knows how to use the language." —Jacques Barzun and Wendell Hertig Taylor

Anna Mary Wells

MURDERER'S CHOICE
"Good writing, ample action, and excellent character work."
—*Saturday Review of Literature*

A TALENT FOR MURDER
"The discovery of the villain is a decided shock." —*Books*

Edward Young

THE FIFTH PASSENGER
"Clever and adroit . . . excellent thriller . . ." —*Library Journal*

Thomas Sterling

☐	P 529	THE EVIL OF THE DAY	$2.25

Julian Symons

☐	P 468	THE BELTING INHERITANCE	$1.95
☐	P 469	BLAND BEGINNING	$1.95
☐	P 481	BOGUE'S FORTUNE	$1.95
☐	P 480	THE BROKEN PENNY	$1.95
☐	P 461	THE COLOR OF MURDER	$1.95
☐	P 460	THE 31ST OF FEBRUARY	$1.95

Dorothy Stockbridge Tillet
(John Stephen Strange)

☐	P 536	THE MAN WHO KILLED FORTESCUE	$2.25

Simon Troy

☐	P 546	SWIFT TO ITS CLOSE	$2.50

Henry Wade

☐	P 543	A DYING FALL	$2.25
☐	P 548	THE HANGING CAPTAIN	$2.25

Hillary Waugh

☐	P 552	LAST SEEN WEARING . . .	$2.50
☐	P 553	THE MISSING MAN	$2.50

Buy them at your local bookstore or use this coupon for ordering:

HARPER & ROW, Mail Order Dept. #PMS, 10 East 53rd St., New York, N.Y. 10022.

Please send me the books I have checked above. I am enclosing $ ________ which includes a postage and handling charge of $1.00 for the first book and 25¢ for each additional book. Send check or money order. No cash or C.O.D.'s please.

Name ____________________

Address ____________________

City ____________ State ____________ Zip ____________

Please allow 4 weeks for delivery. USA and Canada only. This offer expires 1/1/83. Please add applicable sales tax.